Walking to Wonderland

The Duke moved quickly to sit down on the side of Alysia's bed.

He bent forward, meaning to whisper in her ear.

At that moment she opened her eyes and looked up at him.

He thought she was about to give a scream either of horror or perhaps delight.

He bent lower still, and his lips were on hers.

As he touched them, he knew they were just as he had expected they would be—soft, sweet and very innocent.

At first she stiffened, then her arms went round his neck.

It was then he knew that something very strange had happened.

He realised in that second that surprisingly, incredibly, he had fallen in love . . .

A Camfield Novel of Love
by Barbara Cartland

"*Barbara Cartland's novels are all distinguished by their intelligence, good sense, and good nature. . . .*"
— **ROMANTIC TIMES**

"*Who could give be*
going strong than
elist, Barbara Car

Camfield Place,
Hatfield
Hertfordshire,
England

Dearest Reader,

Camfield Novels of Love mark a very exciting era of my books with Jove. They have already published nearly two hundred of my titles since they became my first publisher in America, and now all my original paperback romances in the future will be published exclusively by them.

As you already know, Camfield Place in Hertfordshire is my home, which originally existed in 1275, but was rebuilt in 1867 by the grandfather of Beatrix Potter.

It was here in this lovely house, with the best view in the county, that she wrote *The Tale of Peter Rabbit*. Mr. McGregor's garden is exactly as she described it. The door in the wall that the fat little rabbit could not squeeze underneath and the goldfish pool where the white cat sat twitching its tail are still there.

I had Camfield Place blessed when I came here in 1950 and was so happy with my husband until he died, and now with my children and grandchildren, that I know the atmosphere is filled with love and we have all been very lucky.

It is easy here to write of love and I know you will enjoy the Camfield Novels of Love. Their plots are definitely exciting and the covers very romantic. They come to you, like all my books, with love.

Bless you,

CAMFIELD NOVELS OF LOVE

by Barbara Cartland

A NEW CAMFIELD NOVEL OF LOVE BY

BARBARA CARTLAND

Walking to Wonderland

JOVE BOOKS, NEW YORK

WALKING TO WONDERLAND

A Jove Book / published by arrangement with
the author

PRINTING HISTORY
Jove edition / January 1993

ISBN: 0-515-11021-3

Jove Books are published by The Berkley Publishing Group,
200 Madison Avenue, New York, New York 10016.
The name "JOVE" and the "J" logo
are trademarks belonging to Jove Publications, Inc.

PRINTED IN THE UNITED STATES OF AMERICA

10 9 8 7 6 5 4 3 2 1

Author's Note

HERACLES founded the Olympic Games and fetched from the source of the Danube the wild olive tree whose leaves should crown the victor.

Mankind's first means of transport was by foot, and walking races took place in the Olympic Games held in Athens.

In 1896 a "Marathon" was run to commemorate the legendary feat of a Greek soldier, Phillippides, who, in 490 B.C., ran from Marathon to Athens, a distance of over twenty-two miles.

He did this to warn his countrymen that the Persians had landed a strong force of Cavalry, Infantry, and Archers in Marathon.

In this battle, due to the Greek soldiers, the Greeks were victorious.

Marathons have become a modern road race and

thousands of people take part in them in aid of charity.

They are very popular in England, and when I was in India recently, the Prime Minister, Rajiv Gandhi, was taking part in a Marathon in Delhi.

Walking to Wonderland

chapter one

1827

THE Duke of Eaglefield walked out through the long window of the Banqueting-Room and into the garden.

He moved some distance so that the music he had left behind him was faint.

Then he sat down and looked out to sea.

The stars were coming out overhead and the moon was rising.

In the silver light everything looked very romantic.

The Duke, however, was not looking at the beauty around him.

Sitting on a wooden seat, he was thinking he had escaped from the festivities.

They entranced the King so much that he gave party after party in the Chinese Pavilion at Brighton.

To most people the edifice itself looked fantastic, if out of place.

The contents, valuable though they might be, were definitely inappropriate for England.

A number of them had come down from Carlton House.

They had been discussed, criticised, and laughed at ever since, as Prince Regent, he had spent a fortune on them.

Now, having turned his attention to his house in Brighton, he had spent over a hundred-thousand pounds and he had not yet finished.

The Banqueting-Room, however, where he was entertaining to-night, had been a new addition.

Only the Prince Regent, the Duke had thought, could have imagined anything so fantastic as the enormous chandeliers shaped like waterlilies.

The outside of the Pavilion was supposed to resemble the Kremlin in Moscow.

In the Banqueting-Room, spreading fruity palm trees had a silver dragon peeping through them.

They only resembled, the Duke thought, the dream of somebody who was "not quite right in the head."

He had suddenly felt the heat in which the King always kept his rooms.

Besides which, the chatter and laughter of the women and the incessant intrusion of the Orchestra was more than he could bear.

He therefore escaped when he hoped no one was looking.

Now he drew in deep breaths of the salt air coming from the sea.

If he wanted to be alone, however, he was disappointed.

There were footsteps behind him.

He stiffened, feeling angry at the intrusion.

Then a voice said:

"I thought I saw you slip out, Theo. What are you doing here?"

The Duke gave a sigh of relief.

The intruder was only Harry Hampton, his oldest friend, for whom he had a deep affection.

He and Harry had grown up together. They had played as children.

They had gone to Eton in the same term.

After leaving Oxford, where they were at the same College, they joined the Household Brigade.

The Duke had ceased soldiering, however, after he inherited the title.

But because he missed Harry, he had insisted on him resigning.

Harry sat down on the seat beside the Duke.

Anyone watching them would have thought they were the two best-looking young men they had ever seen.

The Duke, particularly, was outstandingly handsome.

He had dark hair brushed back from a square forehead and classical features.

Harry was fair, but the two men were almost the same size.

Because they were both extremely athletic, there was not an ounce of surplus fat on either of their bodies.

"What made you come out here?" Harry asked. "Was Lady Antonia being tiresome?"

"I was bored," the Duke replied, "bored to tears by the same jokes, the same food, the same music, and, if you want the truth, the same faces!"

Harry laughed.

"I see what you mean," he said. "At the same time, what is the alternative?"

"That is just what I have been asking myself," the Duke answered.

"Somebody must have upset you for you to feel so strongly about it," Harry observed ruminatively. "I saw Lady Antonia being flirtatious with that long-nosed man whose name I cannot remember."

"She is trying to make me jealous," the Duke said, "because she has set her heart on my giving her the pair of chestnuts which I bought a week ago from Penny Wakehurst."

"But you have driven them only once, to my knowledge!" Harry exclaimed.

"I know that," the Duke replied, "but you know what Antonia is like when she shows her greedy claws. She never rests until she has got her own way!"

Harry pressed his lips together to prevent himself saying what he thought of Lady Antonia.

She might be the most beautiful woman in the *Beau Monde*, but she was also undoubtedly one of the most greedy.

He disliked his friend being involved with her.

He had, however, long ago learnt that the Duke never listened to criticism of someone with whom he was enamoured.

Harry therefore decided that the only thing he could do was to wait for the attraction to wear off.

This, where Theo Eaglefield was concerned, invariably happened much sooner than later.

At the same time, he knew that Lady Antonia was,

in his own words, bleeding Theo white.

He disliked her, although it would not be a wise thing to express openly.

Aloud he said:

"I often think that Ladies of Quality are more demanding than the pretty Cyprians. What has happened to Cleone?"

There was a pause before the Duke replied:

"She is sulking because, after I gave her a diamond necklace three weeks ago, I have not yet added the bracelet to match it!"

"Oh, my God!" Harry exclaimed. "Are women never content with what they receive?"

"Not where I am concerned," the Duke answered. "I was thinking just now that all women are interested in is what I can give them."

Harry nodded.

"I suppose that is the truth."

The Duke turned to look at him in surprise.

"You think so too?"

"Of course I do," Harry answered. "You have to admit, Theo, it is part of the penalty for being who you are."

"I do not know what you are saying," the Duke replied.

"Well, I have thought for a long time," Harry said, "that the penalty you pay for being a rich Duke is that the people you meet see only the trappings and not the man beneath them."

The Duke frowned.

"Can that really be true?"

"Of course it is!" Harry replied. "What it amounts to, Theo, is that you see life not as it is, but through a glass window."

The Duke made an impatient gesture, but he did not interrupt.

"How people see you," Harry went on as if he were seeking the right words, "is in a different way from how they see me, or any other ordinary man."

"I do not believe that," the Duke said. "Explain yourself."

"It is quite easy," Harry continued. "They see you through the glass window by which you are protected, as somebody enormously important who owns everything they want themselves—position, money, houses, estates—there is a whole list of them."

"Is that really a fact?" the Duke asked.

"I am afraid so," Harry said. "It is impossible for them to realise that beneath all that there is an ordinary person with feelings like everybody else. And as far as I am concerned, one of the nicest, kindest men in the world!"

The Duke's lips twisted in a smile.

"Thank you, Harry," he said, "but what you are saying is cold comfort."

"Of course it is," Harry admitted. "Unfortunately, Theo, instead of you accepting it all, you are clever enough to realise that you are missing something important."

"What is that?" the Duke asked.

"Knowing the people you meet on equal terms, for one thing."

The Duke stared at him and he went on:

"I have noticed that people talk to you in a different voice from the way they talk to me. How often do you meet anybody who is brave enough to contradict you or tell you that what you are doing is wrong?"

"Why should I be doing anything wrong?" the Duke asked aggressively.

"No one can be right in everything they think and everything they do," Harry answered. "But where you are concerned, they agree with you to your face and grumble about you behind your back."

"I do not believe it!" the Duke replied.

"Think it out for yourself," Harry went on. "Is there anybody else you know who would dare to speak to you as I am doing now?"

There was silence until the Duke said:

"Supposing I admit that you are right, and, incidentally, I am not convinced you are, what do you suggest I do about it?"

"That, again, is something I have thought about," Harry replied, "but I would not have raised the subject unless you had told me how bored you were with women who treat you like a bottomless cornucopia, and men who envy you for what you possess."

The Duke threw up his hands.

"All right," he said, "you need not say any more! I accept that what you are saying has some foundation in fact. But we still get back to the same question—what can I do?"

"I have just been thinking," Harry said, "that you are bored because you are actually always with the same people. If we do not meet them here with His Majesty, then we find them at almost every house at which we are guests in London, or when you entertain them in yours."

"That is true," the Duke conceded somewhat doubtfully.

"On the Race Course you are with the same members of the Jockey Club. If we go to a Mill at Wimbledon, we know exactly who will be there, and the same thing applies to your shooting in the Autumn."

The Duke did not reply.

He knew as Harry spoke that he invariably invited the same guns to shoot at Eagle Hall.

If anyone was left out, they were either hurt or affronted.

"What is more, we hunt with the same pack of hounds," Harry was saying, "and it is well known that if we go to one of the *Maisons de plaisir* around St. James's, the prettiest and most attractive Cyprians are reserved for you."

"Dammit all!" the Duke swore suddenly. "You are making it sound as if my life is not worth living!"

"Of course it is worth living," Harry argued, "but what you are lacking in your daily curriculum is variety."

"Very well," the Duke said sharply, "you provide it! I do not know how to begin."

"As I have been talking to you," Harry said, "I feel as if I was being guided into how I should help you."

"By whom?" the Duke asked cynically.

"I have no idea," Harry said, "but you know how we have often talked of the importance of using one's instincts."

Looking back, the Duke remembered that was one of the subjects on which, as Students, they had argued fiercely at Oxford.

The Duke had, as it happened, always prided himself on having an instinct where the servants were concerned.

If he engaged a man as his Secretary or his Manager, he thought he knew when he first talked to them what they were like.

It was far more reliable than if he had studied their references, however fullsome.

It was also said of him, when he was in the Army, that he had an instinct for what was right and what was wrong.

It was something that would help him if ever he had to face danger.

He had always thought it unfortunate that when he and Harry had joined the Household Brigade, the war was over.

They heard the older men talking of the battles, like Waterloo, in which they had taken part.

He had felt in some strange way that he had been deprived.

War, however unpleasant, was something that would have been important to him in his life.

Aloud he said:

"All right, Harry, I admit I have an instinct where people are concerned."

"That is what is happening now," Harry said, "and your instinct is telling you that Lady Antonia is out for everything she can get, while Cleone is merely greedy because it is her profession to be so."

"And do you really imagine," the Duke asked sarcastically, "that any of the women we have met tonight in that ridiculous Chinese edifice would be any different?"

"Not that lot!" Harry replied scathingly. "They are all the same. To them you are a rich Duke and a very handsome and attractive man! Put those two things together and why should they bother to look any further?"

The Duke laughed as if he could not help it.

"Very well, Harry," he said, "you win. But what do you expect me to do? Explore the world, where I expect once I arrive anywhere, things will be pretty much the same as they are in England, only more uncomfortable?"

He paused before he added:

"I could retire, like a hermit, to Eagle Hall and contemplate my navel in the hope of spiritual salvation!"

"I have a better idea!" Harry said.

There was a note of excitement in his voice which the Duke did not miss.

"It has just come to me again, if you like, through the guidance of your Guardian Angel, or perhaps a lucky star is shining on you. I know what you are to do."

"What is that?" the Duke asked.

He told himself it was certain to be something unpleasant and that this was a ridiculous conversation.

At the same time, he admitted he was intrigued by it.

"I think, in fact, I must make it a bet," Harry said slowly.

"Make what?" the Duke enquired.

"Your chance of meeting ordinary people on an equal footing as a man, and not a Duke."

Turning round on the seat, the Duke looked at him.

"What are you suggesting?" he asked.

Vaguely, at the back of his mind, he was thinking

that if he had to leave England at this particular moment, it was something he had no wish to do.

He had a number of horses at Eagle Hall which he wanted to break in.

He also thought about the pretty woman he had sat next to at dinner.

She had flirted with him in an experienced manner which deserved further exploration.

If he finished with Lady Antonia, and he was sick of her everlasting demands upon his purse, then there was a new face waiting for him.

What the Duke enjoyed in a love-affair was the chase.

He had found from long experience that the end was always the same.

Inevitably, after a very short while, he became bored.

He hated to admit it, even to himself, but all women said the same, thought the same, and behaved in the same way.

Once they were his, he could anticipate every word they were about to say before they spoke.

Every glance they gave him from under their mascaraed eye-lashes he had seen before.

What was really fun was the first approach to a pretty woman who was, inevitably, married.

The question was whether it might be too dangerous to go any further in case her husband created a scandal.

Unfortunately this question, like so many others, was answered far too quickly.

Lady Antonia had a husband who preferred the country to London.

He was often away in the North of England, where he had some property.

Looking back, the Duke could remember that all the women on whom he had bestowed his favours had the same comfortable arrangements.

There was no question, therefore, of a duel being fought at dawn, no question of a jealous husband having him set on by paid assailants.

"What I am doing," Harry was saying very slowly, "is to bet my most treasured black stallion that you have always admired, against your chestnuts, which would be wasted on Lady Antonia, that you could not walk from here to Eagle Hall as an ordinary man and meet ordinary people on the way."

The Duke stared at his friend in astonishment.

"Did you say—walk?" he asked finally.

"I said 'walk'!" Harry said. "And while it is something you have not done seriously since we were at Oxford, you will remember that you did manage to reach the top of Snowdon in rather better trim than anyone else."

"Walk!" the Duke exclaimed. "Why the devil should I do that?"

"Because, my dear Theo," Harry replied, "if you gallop by on one of your superb horses, how can you possibly converse with the ordinary men and women in the streets, in the fields, or, for that matter, in the houses and the Inns in which you will have to stay?"

"I think you have gone off your head!" the Duke said. "How could I possibly walk from here to Eagle Hall, even if I wished to do so?"

"Quite easily," Harry said. "You have two feet to convey you there, and it cannot be much more than fifty miles!"

He calculated for a minute before he added:

"It should not take you more than a week."

"I refuse to do anything so stupid!" the Duke said quickly.

"I thought you would," Harry replied, "so let us go back and you can tell Lady Antonia that she can have your chestnuts. I only hope she is not too rough on them. I never thought her a good driver, or a rider, for that matter."

"I have no intention of giving Antonia the chestnuts!" the Duke said sulkily.

"Personally, I should enjoy owning them," Harry said, "but I might have guessed that all the things you said about wanting *Saracen* were just talk!"

"You know damned well," the Duke said, "I want *Saracen* to serve my mares, while I admit it would deprive you of the one good animal in your stable."

"Very well, try to win him!" Harry challenged the Duke. "But I thought actually it was a forlorn hope that you would do anything so different. You would at least have proved that you are truthful in saying you are bored with the sameness in our lives at the moment. Especially the greed of the people that surround you."

"I agree with that," the Duke said, "but I really cannot see myself walking fifty miles with no one to talk to. And I am quite certain that those Inns to which you refer are damned uncomfortable."

"Of course they are," Harry agreed, "but that is the price you have to pay for not being a rich Duke, puffed up with your own importance and cushioned against anything unpleasant by an army of servants and an ever-increasing crowd of 'Toadies,' who are out to get all they can from you."

"That is not true!" the Duke snapped.

Even as he spoke he knew it was.

He was far too intelligent not to realise that what Harry had been saying was what he had known himself.

He did not put it into words, but it was at the back of his mind.

He could see, almost as if it were laid out in front of him, his life continuing year after year.

It would have a sameness and a lack of excitement.

Anything that was wrong, unpleasant, or dangerous was kept from him by those he employed.

His houses, especially Eagle Hall, were run as if on well-oiled wheels by men he could trust, men who had his best interests at heart.

His Estates were an example to every Landowner, as were his Alms Houses.

His Pensioners blessed him and thanked him for all he did for them.

He was now thinking of introducing Schools into his villages.

The King, when he had made him a Knight of the Garter, had told him that he should be the proudest man in the Kingdom, as few people had a word to say against him.

But if Harry was right—and he was right—then something was missing.

Perhaps it was something called "The Common Touch."

Although he had always believed he had it, he had never tried it out on anybody except the people who surrounded him.

While he was thinking it over seriously, he could hear them saying:

14

"Yes, Your Grace,"—"No, Your Grace,"—"Of course, Your Grace," dozens and dozens of times a day.

His Managers and the Farmers who lived on his farms would say:

"As Your Grace wishes" or "We will do it at once, Your Grace."

There was no opposition, no rebellion, not a voice raised in protest.

Quite suddenly the Duke decided that he would accept Harry's wager, if for nothing else than to show him that he was not afraid of doing something different.

What was more, he would prove that Harry was wrong.

The ordinary people treating him as an ordinary man would be very much the same as those of the *Beau Ton* who treated him as a Duke.

He doubted if the women he met would be less willing to make love to him than Lady Antonia and her predecessors.

"They at least want me as a man!" the Duke said to himself.

Then he was not quite certain if that was correct.

Harry had made him query everything.

Could it be possible that the women who smiled on him beguilingly were in truth looking at his coronet rather than at him?

It was a sobering thought.

Quickly, as if he were afraid that if he waited he might change his mind, he said:

"Very well, Harry, I accept your wager and I hope when I reach Eagle Hall you will be there waiting with *Saracen!*"

Harry let out a cry of delight.

"Do you mean that? Do you really mean it?" he asked.

"Have you ever known me to go back on my word?" the Duke asked.

"You have more guts than I give you credit for," Harry said, "but I have a feeling it will be an experience that you will never regret. It will make you an even nicer person than you are already."

"Shut up!" the Duke exclaimed. "Let us get down to 'brass tacks.' When do I leave? What do I wear? I warn you, if I am bored stiff, I will knock your head off when I reach Eagle Hall!"

"I will risk it," Harry said, "but, curse it, you were always stronger than I am!"

"One thing I have just thought of," the Duke said. "You are not to breathe a word of this to anybody! I have no wish to look a fool, or have half-a-dozen chatterboxes following me to see how I get on."

"Agreed," Harry said quickly. "And, come to think of it, the one person who must not know is your Valet."

The Duke raised his eye-brows.

"Dawson is completely trustworthy."

"I would not trust any servants," Harry said. "Half the gossip that reaches London comes from the Servants' Hall, and as Dawson will obviously think you have gone off your head, he is bound to discuss it with somebody."

"All right," the Duke conceded, "but I can hardly leave dressed in my smartest attire, with Hessian boots and a cravat tied in the very latest fashion!"

Harry laughed.

"No, of course not! If you come to my lodgings

tomorrow morning, I will provide you with some suitable clothes which will be unobtrusive. Then I will drive you out of Town for some distance into the countryside."

His eyes twinkled before he added:

"I will not count that against your fifty miles, but if by any chance you find your feet are tiring and the journey is too wearisome and you either ride or drive the remaining miles home—then the chestnuts are mine!"

"I will see you do not have them unless it is over my dead body!" the Duke retorted.

Harry laughed.

"You are just as sporting as I thought you would be," he remarked. "I only wish that I could come with you. But if I did, we would be laughing and talking, and I doubt if you would be making friends, as I wish you to do, with the Butcher, the Baker or the Candlestickmaker and find out how they will treat you as 'Mr. Field.'"

"Is that what I am to call myself?" the Duke asked curiously.

"Why not? I have always been told that if one is in disguise, it is always a mistake to stray too far from the truth. In an emergency it is difficult to remember an assumed name unless one is familiar with it."

"Very well, as you are the instigator of this ridiculous wager, I will call myself 'Mr. Field,'" the Duke agreed. "Quite a number of my relations have that name, although I am not likely to meet any of them on this trip."

"At any rate, they would not be walking!" Harry remarked.

As the Duke's relatives were all extremely

wealthy, they both laughed at the very idea of it.

Then, as the Duke slipped his arm through Harry's, they walked slowly back towards the lighted rooms of the Chinese Pavilion.

The music grew louder and louder and so did the sound of voices.

Because his mind was on what Harry had planned for him, the Duke thought it would be a mistake, if not a bore, to go back to the crowded room.

Lady Antonia would be waiting for him.

Then he told himself that it would be wrong to do anything out of the ordinary to-night.

Undoubtedly, when he disappeared to-morrow a number of people would be asking what had happened to him.

He told himself he must remember to have a good story ready.

He could always say that he had had to dash away because one of his houses had been damaged by a fire.

In fact, there were any number of reasons why he must leave Brighton.

With a mocking smile he thought to himself that he was already entering into the spirit of the game that Harry had arranged for him.

He knew the whole thing was ridiculous.

Yet some part of his mind recognised it as a challenge.

He felt that if he had refused the suggestion, it would be something he would always regret.

Anyway, it would be admitting that he was fainthearted.

The window by which he had left the Banqueting-Room was still open.

They stepped through it into the crowded room.

There were banners on the walls and furniture which, at enormous expense, the King had had brought from China.

As the Duke looked about him, he saw Lady Antonia and realised she was looking for him.

The one person he thought who must not be aware of what he was going to do would be her.

He had an uncomfortable feeling that somehow, although he had no idea how, she would turn it to her own advantage.

As she saw him and moved towards him, he was forced to admit that she was incredibly beautiful.

At the same time, as he knew only too well, her beauty was "only skin deep."

She reached his side.

"Where have you been?" she asked. "I missed you."

"I found the heat in this room somewhat overpowering," the Duke said, "and outside there is a fresh breeze coming from the sea."

Lady Antonia gave a little shiver of her white shoulders.

"I can take you to a place where we will be both warm and comfortable," she said in a seductive whisper.

There was an expectation in her eyes as she looked up at him which the Duke knew only too well.

Because it was what she expected, and he thought it would be a mistake to do anything different, he made the obvious reply.

"Let me take you home."

"That is what I wanted you to say," she replied softly. "And, darling Theo, I need you!"

"You can listen to what I have to say to you later," the Duke answered in an uncompromising voice.

He escorted her across the room to where King George IV was holding Court.

He was growing enormously fat.

Yet he still had the charm and the good manners which had made him known as "The First Gentleman of Europe."

As the Duke came up to him he held out his hand.

"Eaglefield!" he exclaimed. "I have been wanting to ask your opinion on a new picture I received to-day from Peking. It was expensive, but I am sure you will agree it was worth every penny they were asking for it."

He put a hand on the Duke's shoulder before he went on:

"Come and see it to-morrow, when we can be alone."

"I shall look forward to seeing it with the greatest pleasure," the Duke replied.

Lady Antonia curtsied and the King kissed her hand.

The Duke was thinking that one of the things Harry would have to do for him to-morrow was to make his excuses to the King for his absence.

'It will serve Harry right for getting me into this mess!' the Duke thought.

As he looked round the room his eyes met those of the woman whom he had sat next to at dinner.

There was an obvious invitation in hers.

To accept would mean a scene, and a very violent one, with Antonia, followed by tears and recriminations.

He had been through it all before.

It was a recurrence which he found unpleasant and definitely to be avoided.

He felt Lady Antonia put her hand through his arm and draw him towards the door.

As she did so, he thought, and it seemed incredible, that he was glad, extremely glad, that he had accepted Harry's wager.

chapter two

THE Duke helped Antonia into his comfortable carriage which was waiting outside.

To please the King, of whom he was very fond, he had, like many of his friends, built a house in Brighton.

It was larger and more important-looking than most of the others.

It was at the end of the Stein so that he had a magnificent view of the sea.

He found, however, that it was often a nuisance to have to leave London for Brighton whenever the Monarch decided to visit his Chinese Pavilion.

There was so much going on during what was called "The Season."

This year he had actually hesitated whether he should ignore the pile of invitations on his desk and go to the sea.

The King had, however, assured him that his presence there was essential.

It had been easier to agree than to argue about it.

Lady Antonia did not have a house of her own.

Instead, she rented one from an impoverished Peer.

He preferred the money to the gaieties which inevitably occurred when the King was in residence.

As the carriage drove slowly and sedately towards Lady Antonia's house, she moved nearer to the Duke.

"At last, Dearest," she said, "we are alone, and I am thankful that the King likes everyone to leave early."

She drew closer still.

Her long fingers crept up the Duke's chest and her head rested on his shoulder.

He was aware of the exotic French perfume she used.

The fragrance remained on his body long after he had left her.

He had thought when he first smelt it that it was seductive.

At this moment, however, he found it overpowering.

"I want you, Theo!" Lady Antonia murmured. "I want you wildly, frantically, as no man has ever been wanted before."

The Duke thought cynically that this was something she had said to him before.

He suspected she had said it to a number of men on previous occasions.

"I am sorry, Antonia," he replied, "but I have a

headache, which was why I went outside the Pavilion to get some air. I need to go straight home."

He felt Antonia stiffen with annoyance.

"But you cannot leave me!" she protested. "Just stay for a little while. That will make me very happy."

The Duke knew exactly what she meant by "a little while."

He had no intention of walking back to his house just as dawn was breaking.

"Forgive me, Antonia," he replied, "but I really feel I must rest and hope this headache will be gone by morning."

"I will soothe your head," Lady Antonia replied. "I will make you a tisane which will take away all your pain."

The Duke had drunk one of Lady Antonia's tisanes before.

He knew they were by no means a soothing mixture.

They were, in fact, some sort of Oriental aphrodisiac which she had imported to England.

He did not speak.

A few seconds later the horses came to a standstill outside her house.

The footman got down from the Box to open the door.

"Good-night, Antonia," the Duke said.

She was leaning towards the open door and now, when he spoke, she moved back to sit down beside him again.

"You cannot really mean you are driving on without saying good-night to me?" she asked in a low voice.

"That was my intention," the Duke replied.

"Then I think it is extremely rude as well as very unkind of you!"

The Duke did not answer, and after a moment she added:

"If you persist in treating me in such an unchivalrous manner, I shall just stay here!"

There was a note in her voice which told the Duke that was exactly what she would do.

Because he had no wish to have a scene in front of his servants, he knew he must capitulate.

"Very well," he sighed, "I will come in and say good-night to you and the carriage can wait."

He started to alight, and there was a glint of triumph in Antonia's eyes.

She rose again to step out onto the pavement.

By this time her Night-footman had opened the front-door.

When the Duke followed Lady Antonia into the Hall, he shut it behind them.

Lady Antonia was already moving up the stairs when the Duke said:

"Let us go into the Sitting-Room."

As he spoke he walked towards the Sitting-Room, which was at the back of the house.

The Drawing-Room was on the First Floor.

For a moment Lady Antonia hesitated.

Then she thought that if she walked on up the stairs the Duke would leave the house and she could do nothing to stop him.

With a hard look in her eyes she came down and crossed the Hall.

The Duke was already in the Sitting-Room, standing with his back to the fireplace.

The tapers in the chandeliers had been extinguished.

There were, however, two candelabra still alight which illuminated the room.

Lady Antonia came in and slammed the door behind her.

Then she walked slowly towards the Duke, saying:

"What is all this about? Why are you behaving in this extraordinary manner?"

"It is not particularly extraordinary," the Duke contradicted. "As I have told you, Antonia, I wish to go home to bed—and alone!"

"That is something I have never known you to want to do since I first loved you!" Lady Antonia snapped.

She paused before she said slowly:

"If it is that woman Christina whom you were sitting next to at dinner, I swear I will scratch her eyes out and make you sorry you were ever born!"

The Duke was watching the way her face contorted as she spoke.

He thought that when she was angry she was actually ugly.

It was then he knew that once again the curtain had fallen at the end of yet another of his love-affairs.

It was something which had happened a great number of times, but never quite so suddenly or so completely.

He knew that Lady Antonia no longer held any attraction for him.

Even if she had stood before him naked, as she had often done before, he would not have felt the slightest desire to touch her.

Aloud he said:

"You are being both hysterical and ridiculous, Antonia! I have never met the woman you are talking about before to-night. I did not even speak to her after the dinner was over."

"Then who is it?" Lady Antonia demanded. "It must be someone who is making you behave in this monstrous fashion!"

"No one," the Duke argued. "And I am prepared to swear to it by everything I hold sacred."

"I do not believe you! You are lying!" Lady Antonia said accusingly.

The Duke walked towards the door.

"You are behaving like a spoilt child," he said, "and if you do not believe what I tell you, there is nothing I can do about it. Good-night!"

He opened the door as he spoke and moved into the Hall.

The Night-footman, realising he was leaving, opened the front-door.

As the Duke walked out into the night he heard a shriek from behind him.

Lady Antonia came running out.

"How dare you demean me like this, Theo!" she screamed. "I will not allow you to do so!"

The Duke did not turn round.

He merely stepped into his carriage.

As the footman hurriedly climbed up on the Box, the Coachman, anticipating his Master's wishes, drove away.

The Duke did not look back.

If he had done so he would have seen Lady Antonia stamping her foot in fury and frustration.

She was swearing abuse at the Night-footman

as she went upstairs to bed.

As he drove on, the Duke asked himself how he could have been such a fool as to fall for a woman who, when upset, could behave like a Billingsgate fishwife.

Where women were concerned, the Duke was extremely fastidious.

He was very easily put off by anything that was in the least vulgar.

He disliked women who used too many *double entendres* in their conversation, and those who wooed a man with whom they were enamoured.

He preferred that men should do the wooing both in bed and outside.

As far as the Beauties with whom he had been infatuated were concerned, it was the small, unexpected things that finally made him lose interest in them.

One Beauty—and she was beautiful—had an irritating habit of twisting the rings on her fingers all the time she talked to him.

Another, he decided, was too voluptuous in the way she behaved.

A third would do everything to make him stay with her when his inclination was to leave.

Trivial things, but irritating as they brought the curtain down on yet another *affaire de coeur*.

Now he wondered why he had not realised sooner how very unrestrained and undignified Lady Antonia could be.

He realised that what she was feeling was jealousy.

She was obviously aware that he had not been wholeheartedly attentive towards her recently.

Yet there had been no one else.

As his Valet came to help him undress, the Duke was thinking perhaps it was a good thing that he was going away.

Thank goodness, to-night, at any rate, he would have a rest and be undisturbed until the morning.

Yet when he was alone in the darkness he asked himself if he was crazy to have accepted Harry's ridiculous wager.

He could easily have stayed in Brighton, where there was a great number of his friends.

He could, of course, have gone to Eagle Hall in his carriage to ride his new horses.

Now Brighton was barred because of Lady Antonia.

Yet he was not prepared to surrender his chestnuts to Harry without a struggle.

He knew quite well that Harry had more or less goaded him into taking the wager.

He had a deep fondness for Harry, as Harry had for him.

They had always been as much a part of each other's lives as if they had been brothers.

Harry's parents lived only a short distance from Eagle Hall.

The two boys had shared everything between them.

It was only now, when they were both twenty-eight, that they had different tastes in women.

The Duke was aware that Harry had always rather scoffed at the outstanding Society Beauties.

He said, quite truthfully, they had been spoilt by too much admiration.

Now he was admitting that Harry was right.

It was doubtless due to too much admiration that Antonia had come to believe that every man was her slave.

'I am well rid of her!' the Duke thought as he turned over on his pillow.

*   *   *

Dawson called the Duke at eight o'clock.

Having had a substantial breakfast, he then went to see Harry in his lodgings.

Harry could have afforded to rent a house.

Alternatively, he could have accepted the Duke's invitation to stay with him.

"I think, Theo," he had said when the Duke had asked him, "it would be best for me to be on my own. You may have visitors who would stay with you. They might feel embarrassed if I were there, and the same applies where I am concerned."

The Duke knew exactly what he was implying.

If Antonia's husband turned up unexpectedly, she would undoubtedly meet him secretly at his house.

It was something of which he did not approve.

But it was wise to be prepared for every contingency.

Harry was therefore lodging in a very comfortable house run admirably by a couple who had been Cook and Butler to several of the Quality.

They knew exactly how to treat a Gentleman.

There were only a few other people in the house.

One was an old lady of ninety who had come to Brighton to die.

One other, a young man like himself, was seldom to be found anywhere except in the Royal Pavilion.

Harry was waiting for the Duke, and when he appeared he said:

"Good-morning, Theo! Have you changed your mind?"

"Certainly not!" the Duke retorted. "I gave my word and you know you can rely on it."

Harry's eyes twinkled.

He was quite sure that the Duke had quarrelled with Lady Antonia last night.

He was, however, too tactful to mention it.

"Now, what we have to decide," he said in his most businesslike manner, "is what you are to wear. It is unnecessary for me to tell you that you are far too smart to look like an ordinary man who is walking because he cannot afford a horse."

"If you think that I am going to be penniless on this ridiculous exercise," the Duke replied, "you are very much mistaken!"

"You can take any money you like," Harry replied. "At the same time, remember, it might be stolen from you. But I doubt if a Highwayman would think you looked rich enough to be of any interest to him."

The Duke did not answer.

Harry went into his bed-room, saying:

"Come and see what I have laid out for you."

The Duke had been dressed by Dawson and looked exceedingly smart.

He wore a cut-away coat which fitted without a wrinkle.

This had been decreed by the arbiter of fashion, Beau Brummell, before—eleven years ago—he had been forced into exile.

The Duke's drainpipe trousers, which fitted under

his feet by means of an elastic band, were exceedingly smart.

So, too, was his champagne-coloured waist-coat.

His spotlessly white starched muslin cravat was tied in an enigmatic fashion.

It had been the envy of every young Beau when he arrived in Brighton.

Looking at him, Harry knew that if he walked down the Stein, as was fashionable at midday, he would attract more attention than the King himself.

"Now, what you have to appear is more or less anonymous," he was saying, "so I am going to try to make you look far more ordinary than you do at the moment."

Harry picked up from the bed a pair of trousers that, while well-cut, were an indeterminate shade of dark brown.

The Duke looked at them and gave a little shudder.

"I dislike those!" he said.

"Put them on," Harry commanded. "It does not matter how they look to you, but how you appear to the people who see you."

Because there was no point in arguing, the Duke put them on.

He could not imagine why Harry had ever bought such a dull colour.

However, they fitted him quite well.

He could therefore give no reason why he should not wear them.

Instead of his cut-away coat there was a black one with a full skirt which was no longer fashionable in London.

It was still worn by older men.

The Duke was certain, because it was slightly worn, that it would not attract any attention.

There was a plain waist-coat of the same colour as the trousers, and without being told to, the Duke took off his smart cravat.

Harry handed him a long silk tie which was the colour of burgundy and which again had been well-worn.

"Just twist it over," he said.

There were no high peaking points to the collar above his chin.

The Duke was dressed very much like a middle-class businessman, or perhaps a Gentleman down on his luck.

"I suppose I am to be allowed a hat?" he asked somewhat sarcastically.

"Of course," Harry said.

He brought one from a cupboard, and the Duke laughed.

It was a broadly-crowned high hat which he knew had been worn earlier in the century.

It had been discarded some years ago by all the Bucks of St. James's Street.

He put it on his head, and Harry exclaimed:

"Perfect!"

"What I want to know," the Duke remarked, "is where you got all these peculiar clothes from?"

"You will hardly believe it," Harry answered, "but my Landlady had a son who died six years ago. He had been doing well and was in business on his own in London."

"What did he die of?" the Duke asked suspiciously.

"Nothing infectious," Harry said quickly. "He

had an accident and the Doctors treating him made a mess of it which, as you know, they usually do, and it killed him."

"And his mother kept his clothes."

"She had them all neatly packed up in camphor balls," Harry said, "and I borrowed them from her. She wishes to have them back as soon as you have finished with them."

The Duke laughed.

"Ingenious, Harry! I have to commend you! Your organisation is superb!"

"That is what I think myself," Harry said, "and you do look entirely different, Theo."

He picked up a bag from the corner of the bedroom.

It was quite a cheap one, made of a light material with a strap that could be worn over the shoulder.

The Duke looked at it curiously.

"This bag contains," Harry said, "two shirts, two pairs of stockings, two handkerchiefs, a brush and comb and a set of razors."

"I would never have thought of it," the Duke laughed.

"I guessed that!" Harry answered. "And to save yourself any trouble, you can throw away your shirts when they are dirty."

"An extravagant idea," the Duke remarked mockingly.

"You can afford it," Harry replied.

He looked out of the window.

The sun was shining on the sea.

It was still too early for there to be anybody about on the Stein.

But they both knew that in another couple of hours

the whole place would be crowded.

"Come on," Harry said, "I have my Chaise outside, and I will drive you to your starting-point."

"I suppose I should be grateful for that!" the Duke said grudgingly. "Take care of my clothes. Dawson will be furious if you mess them up when I have need of them again."

"You know full well that before I leave in a week's time for Eagle Hall," Harry said, "I will tell Dawson you have sent a message for me to pack up and join you there."

"How do you intend to account for my absence when I do not put in an appearance later to-day?" the Duke asked.

"I will tell Dawson, and anybody else who is interested," Harry replied, "and that includes a 'certain Lady,' that while you were with me a messenger came to tell you you were wanted immediately at Newmarket."

"At Newmarket?" the Duke questioned.

"Two of your horses have been taken mysteriously ill, but your Trainer said it would be a great mistake for it to be known publicly, as it would doubtless affect their running at the next meeting."

"Harry, you are a genius!" the Duke said. "Only you could think up such a ridiculous, but credible, reason for my absence."

"Thank you," Harry replied with modesty.

"Oh, and by the way," the Duke went on, "I am expected at the Pavilion some time to-day. You had better tell the King that story as soon as possible. He always likes to be 'in the know' before it is common knowledge."

Harry nodded.

He knew His Majesty's idiosyncrasies as well as the Duke did.

They went downstairs and outside to where Harry's Chaise was waiting.

It was a very comfortable one, drawn by four horses.

The Duke got in quickly as Harry told his groom he was not wanted.

Picking up the reins, he drove off.

There was no one to notice them as they drove down the almost empty streets and were soon in the country.

There were the Downs rolling away on one side of them.

The dust rose behind their wheels in a cloud which the Duke thought could be very concealing.

"I thought you could start from the Sail and Anchor," Harry said.

It was a well known Inn about three miles outside Brighton.

It was also in the right direction for him to take if he was to travel from Sussex into Surrey.

Then he would go on to Berkshire, where Eagle Hall was situated.

"I think you are being rather mean," the Duke replied, "in taking me so short a way. I am thinking I shall be pretty footsore by the time I reach home."

"I shall be waiting to see you come stumbling in," Harry said, "and at least you will have done what none of our other friends could possibly achieve because they are too lazy."

"Promise you will tell no one what I am doing," the Duke insisted.

"I am not going to answer that," Harry replied,

"because it is insulting. This is an arrangement we have made between ourselves, and if anybody else gets to hear about it, it will not be *my* fault!"

"Nor mine," the Duke said. "I am only thinking how they would laugh if they could see me now— that is—if they recognised me!"

Harry thought the Duke was being mock-modest.

He was so handsome and so well-built that he was quite certain his friends would know him, whatever he was wearing.

However, he thought it a mistake to say so. He drove on until the Sail and Anchor came in sight.

He drew in his horses so that they moved a little slower.

"Now, listen, Theo," he said. "If things should go wrong, although I cannot imagine why they should, do not be a fool. Hire a horse and ride straight to Eagle Hall."

The Duke looked at him in surprise.

"What do you imagine could go wrong?" he asked. "You said yourself that I am of no interest to any Highwayman. I cannot imagine there is any other sort of danger in the quiet lanes of England."

"No, of course not," Harry agreed. "At the same time, I started this and I have no wish for there to be any repercussions from it."

The Duke brought his hand down on his friend's knee.

"You started it," he said, "and I intend to see it through, but I have been asking myself ever since how I can be such a damned fool as to have listened to you!"

Harry drew up his horses outside the Sail and Anchor.

There were no visitors at that hour of the morning.

The doors appeared to be firmly locked.

"Good-bye, Harry!" the Duke said cheerfully as he got out of the carriage. "I shall be thinking as I walk along, doubtless getting corns on my toes, how much I will enjoy riding *Saracen!*"

"'Do not count your chickens before they are hatched!'" Harry quoted. "And take care of yourself, old man!"

He turned his horses.

As he drove past him, the Duke swept off his hat with a mockingly exaggerated bow.

As the dust obscured the horses and Harry, he started to walk along the road.

He was thinking as he did so he must have "bats in his belfry" to ever have agreed to this ridiculous wager.

He walked on until at midday he began to feel hungry.

Harry had been right in thinking that except when he was out shooting, he had done very little walking.

There were so many excellent horses in his stable.

Riding was exercise of one kind, making love another.

But walking was something different.

The Duke was relieved when he saw ahead of him a small black and white Inn.

It stood on the traditional village green in the middle of which there was a duck-pond.

He walked across the green and sat down on a bench outside the Inn.

In front of it there was a wooden table.

The Landlord appeared almost at once.

"Anythin' Oi can get ye?" he asked.

"It depends what you can offer me," the Duke replied. "And, as it happens, I am extremely hungry."

"Well, ye looks a foin upstandin' man," the Landlord said, "an' Oi' thinks wot ye'd loik t'eat is some slices o' 'am, roast beef an' onion. Th' cheese be just as ripe as it should be!"

"Excellent!" the Duke answered.

"An' wot'll ye 'ave t'drink?" the Landlord asked. "Oi've got ale or cider. Ye won't get much else in this part o' the world."

"Cider would suit me best," the Duke replied.

The Landlord went into the Inn.

A few minutes after he came back with the beef and ham he had described.

The beef was somewhat tough, but the Duke was hungry.

The ham, which was home-cured, was excellent.

On the plate were several cold potatoes, some fresh lettuce leaves, and pickled onions.

The cheese was, in fact, over-ripe, but the Duke ate it.

He was more appreciative of the newly-baked bread which the Landlord had placed on the table with a large pat of butter.

Having finished, the Duke paid the Landlord what seemed to him to be an extraordinarily small amount for quite a good meal.

As the Landlord took the money he asked:

"Do you have many visitors here?"

"Sometimes yes, an' sometimes no," the Landlord said. "It's a tricky business keepin' an Inn these days wi' most people too poor to afford t' drink more than once a week."

"Is that true?" the Duke asked in surprise. "I thought the troubles that occurred when the war was over were now at an end."

"Th' 'arvest weren't too good last year," the Inn-Keeper replied, "an' wi' the King spendin' so much money on frivolities an' fancy buildin's as moight 'ave come out of a nightmare, the Tax Collectors is busy makin' th' loiks of us pay for it!"

The Duke thought he was on dangerous ground, and got to his feet.

"Well, best of luck to you," he said, "and I hope things will improve in the country in the future."

"Oi doubts it," the Landlord said grimly. "An' a young fella loik yerself shouldn't be walkin' about wi'out havin' a job. That's wot be wrong in t'country—there's b'aint enough jobs to go round."

"I agree with you there," the Duke said. "Well, good-bye."

He thought the King's extravagance in building the Chinese Pavilion at Brighton was a bad example to the whole country.

With Napoleon defeated, there had been two years when the Farmers in England had suffered terribly.

Cheap food had begun to come into the country, so that their crops were not wanted.

The Country Banks closed their doors.

A great many people lost everything they possessed.

The Duke realised that in London nobody seemed to care.

There were extravagant parties every night, especially at Carlton House.

The Prince Regent's debts had increased dramatically every year.

41

He wondered whether people like himself should have done something about it.

He and Harry had joined the Household Brigade and had not really understood what was happening in rural England.

He walked on, thinking that Harry would be pleased at the conversation he had had with the Proprietor of the Inn.

He thought about it later that night when he stopped at an Inn about six o'clock and ate some supper.

His legs were aching and, as the place was clean, he asked for a bed.

He got into it as the sun went down and instantly fell asleep.

When he woke next morning he could not believe he could have slept so well.

'Harry will laugh,' he thought.

After a breakfast of eggs and bacon he set off.

He passed two yokels, one driving a few sheep, the other with some cows in front of him.

Just occasionally there was a farm-cart drawn by a tired horse, with a sleepy old man holding the reins.

It was then he was aware that on his right there was a river.

He left the road to walk across the fields towards it.

It was not a wide river, but it was quite deep.

There were willow trees hanging over it and occasionally a wild duck or a Kingfisher to attract his attention.

It was certainly more interesting than the dusty road.

He moved on, and the river widened.

It was also moving swiftly and he wondered why.

Then he saw that just ahead there was a small cascade.

Beyond it was a weir in a state of disrepair, and he looked at it curiously.

Then, as he rounded a clump of bushes growing beside it, there was a deep pool.

A young woman was standing on the very edge of it, looking down into the depths of what he imagined was a whirlpool.

The Duke looked once again into the water.

Then he glanced again at the girl, who was some feet away from him.

He had a sudden horrifying thought, but he could hardly believe it.

His instinct told him that she intended to throw herself into the swirling darkness beneath her.

chapter three

THE Duke hesitated.

The girl put her hands together as if she were praying and looked up at the sky.

He was sure she was going to take one step forward and fall into the water.

He moved a little closer as he said:

"That would be an extremely stupid thing to do!"

She started and gave a cry.

Instinctively she moved backwards as she looked at him.

He saw that she was extremely lovely.

She had very large, frightened eyes in a small face, and fair hair that seemed like a halo.

"Go . . . away!" she exclaimed, and her voice was low and frightened.

"I have an idea," the Duke said slowly, "that you intend to fall into that dark, unpleasant-looking water beneath you. I do beg you to do nothing of the sort."

"It . . . it is none . . . of your . . . business," the girl stammered. "Go . . . away! I want . . . to be . . . alone."

"If you do anything so foolish," the Duke continued, "I shall be obliged to play the hero and, as this is the only suit I possess, I have no wish to look like a wet dog."

The girl gave a deep sigh before she said:

"I cannot . . . think why . . . you should . . . interfere. I had no idea . . . anyone was . . . here . . . and . . . now . . . "

"Now you are beginning to think again about doing something utterly absurd. I can assure you that however difficult it may be, life is very precious."

As the Duke spoke, he thought it was a strange thing for him to say.

Yet he could think of nothing more wrong and wicked than that this child—she seemed little more—should deliberately end her life.

He realised she was trembling, and he said after a moment:

"I tell you what we will do. We will sit down under the trees and you can tell me why you should want to do anything so appalling as to end your life. If you can convince me that it is the right thing to do, then I will go on my way without saying any more."

The girl hesitated.

He had the idea that she was wondering whether she should defy him and throw herself, there and then, into the whirlpool.

To stop her, he put out his hand to take hers.

"Come," he said in an authoritative tone. "I have put my proposition, and you must acquiesce to it."

He had somehow sapped her willpower.

She let him draw her from the edge of the whirlpool and along the side of the river.

Just ahead of them there was a clump of trees.

Still holding her hand, the Duke led her towards them.

When they reached the trees he released her.

He sat down on the soft grass which was slightly raised from that on the side of the river.

After a moment's indecision the girl followed him.

The skirt of her muslin gown billowed out as she sank onto the grass.

Looking at her, the Duke thought it impossible for anyone to be so beautiful.

She did, in fact, look like a very young angel who had fallen out of Heaven by mistake.

His experienced eye was also aware that the gown she was wearing was expensive.

He also saw that round her long neck there was a string of perfect pearls.

She was not looking at him, but out across the river.

He was sure she was seeing nothing but her own troubles.

"Now, tell me," he said in his most beguiling voice, "why you have come here to end what has been a very short life."

"There is . . . nothing . . . else I can . . . do," the girl answered.

"Let us start from the beginning," the Duke suggested. "What is your name?"

"Alysia."

"Mine is Theo," he said. "Theo Field."

She turned her face towards him before she said:

"I am sure you must have been christened Theo-dore."

The Duke was surprised.

"Why should you think that?"

"Because it is Greek, and I expect if you had used the whole name at school you would have been teased about it."

The Duke was astonished.

It was true that before he went to Eton he called himself "Theo" and insisted that everybody else did the same.

But not one woman he had known since he had grown up had suggested that it was short for Theodore, nor that the name itself was Greek.

"You are right in what you have just said," he replied after a few seconds. "But I am interested to know how you should be aware that my name is Greek."

"My Father was a . . . Don at Cambridge, and a Professor of Languages," Alysia answered. "As he taught students Greek, of which he was particularly fond, he also taught me."

"And your Father approves of what you are now contemplating?" the Duke asked.

"Papa is . . . dead," Alysia answered. "I promise you there is . . . nothing else . . . I can . . . do."

There was a note of despair in her voice that the Duke did not miss.

"That is what I am waiting for you to tell me," he said, "so start at the beginning."

As he spoke, he saw her glance back the way she had come.

He knew she was afraid that if it took too long to tell him what he wished to know, somebody might appear.

They would prevent her from drowning herself.

He was not certain how he knew what she was thinking.

He was pretty sure that this was the truth.

"There is . . . nothing . . . else I can . . . do," she repeated. "I . . . swear to . . . you there is . . . nothing else."

"But you must convince me," the Duke said, "otherwise I shall have to try to find your family whom you have left to come here."

"No, no! You must . . . not do . . . that! That is . . . something . . . you—"

She stopped.

Clasping her hands together, she said:

"I . . . I will tell you everything . . . then you will . . . understand."

"That is what I am waiting to hear," the Duke said.

He leaned back against a tree-trunk as she spoke.

This was certainly a very unusual occurrence and something which had never happened to him before.

"Papa, who . . . as I . . . told you, was a Don . . . at Cambridge, ran away with . . . my Mother and they were very . . . very happy."

There was a sob in her voice before with an effort she continued:

"Then Papa was . . . killed while riding. It . . . broke my Mother's heart and . . . she was . . . desperately . . . unhappy."

"Surely you helped her?" the Duke murmured.

"I . . . I tried to," Alysia said, "but she just wanted to d-die and be with . . . Papa."

Her voice sounded choked in her throat, and the Duke knew she was fighting back the tears.

"What happened?" he asked.

"A . . . man came to . . . our house . . . unexpectedly who had known . . . Mama and Papa in the . . . past. He asked Mama to . . . marry him!"

"Surely that was somewhat precipitate?" the Duke asked somewhat cynically.

"It did not . . . happen at . . . once," Alysia said. "I am telling this . . . very badly . . . but Miles Maulcroft—that is . . . his name—came day after day, bringing Mama presents, flattering her, until in . . . the end she . . . finally agreed to . . . marry him."

Now there was an expression of horror in Alysia's large eyes as she said:

"He is horrible . . . a man I . . . mistrusted from the first moment I . . . saw him!"

"But your Mother married him," the Duke said quietly.

"Yes . . . she married him . . . and I suppose in a way he made her a little . . . h-happier because she was no longer . . . alone."

Alysia put her hand up over her eyes as if she could not bear to think of it.

Once again, as if she was frightened that time was passing, she looked over her shoulder at the green fields rolling away into the distance.

There was no one in sight, and the Duke said gently:

"Go on! What happened after that?"

"Mama d-died . . . she got weaker . . . and weaker . . . and now . . . I am almost . . . certain that my . . . Stepfather . . . murdered her!"

The Duke stiffened and sat upright.

"Did he really do that? How did he do such a thing—and why?"

"I began to . . . suspect him after . . . Mama had died and he found she had . . . left all her . . . money to me!"

"You really believe he killed her?"

"I remember Mama, when she was ill, saying to me that he always carried in her food to the bed-room. And once . . . I am almost certain I saw him . . . adding something to . . . a dish outside . . . her door."

"It seems incredible," the Duke exclaimed, "if he loved her!"

"When he started . . . raging at me . . . after Mama's Will had been . . . read, I knew that . . . all he had . . . really wanted was her . . . money. He has . . . none of his . . . own, and of course . . . while he was . . . living in our house, he . . . did not have to . . . pay for . . . anything."

"You say your Mother was rich?"

"Very rich, but she had made . . . a Will with . . . the best solicitors in the whole of Brighton. In fact, I think the . . . King himself . . . employs them."

"And she left everything to you?"

"Everything!" Alysia agreed. "My Stepfather was . . . furiously angry when he found that all he could . . . obtain was . . . enough money to keep up . . . the house and provide for me. But he also realised something . . . else."

"What was it?" the Duke enquired.

"That that was . . . all he could obtain . . . until I . . . married!"

The Duke looked puzzled.

"I am sure that meant that your money would go

to your husband, and your Stepfather would get nothing."

"Yes, he knew that . . . which is why he has arranged a . . . marriage for me."

The Duke began to realise what had happened, but he waited until Alysia continued:

"He has found an . . . impoverished Peer who . . . lives not far . . . from here. His house is . . . tumbling down and his Estate grows . . . nothing but . . . weeds. I know from what I . . . heard him say that if . . . Lord Gosforde marries me he will give my . . . Stepfather half . . . my fortune!"

"I suppose," the Duke said slowly, "you have refused to marry this man?"

"Of course I have . . . refused," Alysia answered. "He is old . . . getting on for . . . sixty and . . . horrible! I would die rather . . . than let him . . . touch me!"

"So that is why you came to the whirlpool?"

"There was . . . a man," Alysia replied, "who had . . . drunk too much . . . and who drowned here last . . . year. It was a . . . long time before they . . . found the . . . body."

"There must be something else you can do?" the Duke said.

"I have . . . thought and . . . thought," Alysia said, "and if I . . . run away . . . I have . . . nowhere to . . . go."

"What about your Mother's family?"

"They were very angry when she married Papa and they live in the North of England . . . somewhere near . . . Liverpool. I have . . . no way of . . . reaching . . . them."

The Duke thought that people who were very rich

and lived in Liverpool had usually made their money from the Slave Trade.

It was something which he abhorred.

He, however, asked:

"What do you mean—you have no money?"

"My Stepfather never gives me . . . anything with which to . . . buy what I . . . need. He pays . . . any bills that I incur and . . . begrudges me even the . . . price of a new gown. He makes it very clear that he . . . wants the . . . money for . . . himself."

"I do see it is an appalling situation," the Duke said. "And you cannot marry this man Gosforde."

"I know," Alysia said, "that is why the . . . only thing I can . . . do is to . . . drown myself."

The Duke was trying to remember if he had ever heard of Lord Gosforde.

If he was old and impoverished, it was unlikely.

Anyway, he could understand this lovely girl's predicament.

Her horror at the idea of being tied to a man who was old enough to be her grandfather was obvious.

"Are you quite certain," he asked, "that you cannot persuade your Stepfather to forget the idea of this marriage if your Solicitors could give you a little more money from your Mother's fortune?"

"I think Mama had discovered how avaricious my Stepfather is. Perhaps she even suspected that he was trying to murder her. She made the Will soon . . . after she began . . . to feel . . . ill."

"It does not seem possible that any man could behave in such a way," the Duke said abruptly.

"My Stepfather is determined . . . absolutely determined that I shall marry Lord Gosforde. When I told him I refused to do so, he told me he would whip me insensible if I did not agree."

The Duke drew in his breath.

He could not imagine any man who was not the worst kind of brute beating anything so small and fragile.

Alysia was as beautiful as a flower just coming into bloom.

Quite suddenly he knew what he must do.

He rose to his feet and put out his hand to help Alysia to hers.

"Now, you . . . understand," she said, "are you . . . leaving me?"

"On the contrary," the Duke said. "I am going on my way, and you are coming with me!"

She looked at him in surprise.

"C-coming . . . with . . . you?"

"I have a long way to walk. At the end of it, I know of an elderly lady who will be delighted to have you with her and that will give us time to consider what you can do in the future."

He was thinking of his Grandmother, who lived in the Dower House on his Estate.

She was growing old, but she liked young people round her.

He was quite certain she would welcome Alysia and find a place for her in her household.

Perhaps she could be a Reader, as his Grand-mother's eyes were beginning to fail.

He was aware that Alysia was looking up at him as if she could not believe what she had heard.

"Do you . . . mean . . . that? Do you . . . really mean . . . it?" she asked.

"Of course I mean it!" the Duke said. "You cannot expect me to walk on and leave you here to die. It is a sunny day and there will be, I am sure, a great number of adventures ahead of us."

Alysia gave an unsteady little laugh.

"How can . . . you be . . . so kind . . . how can you . . . suggest such an . . . idea when you have . . . only just . . . met . . . me?"

"I would much prefer to take you with me than let you plunge into that murky water in your nice gown."

He spoke in a way that made it sound ridiculous, and Alysia whispered:

"Thank you . . . oh, thank you for being . . . so kind to me. I was so . . . afraid you were intent on . . . taking me back home . . . but I felt if I could run away he would . . . not be . . . able to find me."

"I have not run since I was at School," the Duke said, "but I should be very ashamed of myself if I could not catch a small butterfly like you!"

Alysia gave another little laugh.

Then she said:

"You really . . . mean it? It will not be . . . a nuisance for . . . you to . . . take me with you . . . to the . . . kind lady of whom you spoke?"

"It is what I intend to do," the Duke said, "and I have a feeling that the sooner we are on our way, the better!"

"Yes . . . of course," Alysia said. "They may . . . discover soon . . . that I am no . . . longer in the . . . house and, as I am not riding, my . . . Stepfather will . . . wonder where . . . I am."

She gave a little shiver as she said:

"Suppose he . . . catches up with . . . us? He might . . . hurt . . . you. He is a . . . very violent . . . man!"

"I expect I would be able to deal with him," the

Duke replied, "but, as I dislike fisticuffs of any sort, I suggest we hurry to a place where he is not likely to search for us."

"Yes . . . yes . . . of course," Alysia agreed.

She started to move beside the Duke over the short grass.

He thought that the sooner they were as far away as possible from her home, the better. So he moved quickly.

They must have walked for a mile before the Duke was aware that Alysia was struggling to keep up with him.

Her breath was coming quickly from between her lips.

Her face was a little flushed.

The wind had blown her hair into little curls around her forehead.

She looked lovely and even more like the Angel he had imagined her to be.

He began to realise that to be accompanied by anyone so attractive would undoubtedly cause comment.

He did not, however, say very much until he was hungry.

It was then he saw ahead of them some thatched roofs.

By keeping near the river, they had now reached a village.

"I can see houses ahead," the Duke remarked. "I am sure there will be an Inn where we can get something to eat."

Alysia hesitated.

"I know this village," she said. "I have sometimes ridden through it, and it is not very far from home."

There was an undoubted touch of fear in her voice as she added:

"I . . . I might be recognised."

The Duke thought this was extremely likely.

There could hardly be many girls as beautiful as Alysia in the neighbourhood.

"You need not come into the village. Wait in the wood just outside, where you will not be seen. I will get the food and we can have a picnic."

"I am sure that would be . . . uncomfortable for . . . you," Alysia answered. "It would be . . . better if you . . . ate in the Inn, then brought me . . . something . . . perhaps a sandwich."

"Leave it to me," the Duke replied. "We must be practical in case by this time your Stepfather is looking for you."

Alysia glanced behind her, as he had noticed her doing several times as they were walking.

"I am sure he will expect me to be . . . hiding in the garden or the woods," she said. "He has always disliked me, but, because he . . . intends me to marry Lord Gosforde, he has lately . . . insisted that I have my meals with him and he . . . locks me in . . . my room . . . at night."

"How did you escape to-day?" the Duke enquired.

"I got up very early, tied a sheet to my balcony, and climbed down it to the garden. It was foolhardy, but I managed it. I ran down to the river, concealing myself as I went in the shrubs and trees so that nobody saw me."

The Duke smiled.

"That was clever of you."

"I was desperate! Lord Gosforde was coming to dinner this evening, and I know my Stepfather and he were going to plan the wedding."

"And when was that to be?" the Duke asked.

"To-morrow, or the next day. My Stepfather wants money desperately and will not wait any longer."

The Duke could see the whole problem being thought out between the two unscrupulous men.

If, as Alysia thought, Miles Maulcroft had killed her Mother, he would not hesitate to kill her if she made too much trouble for him.

Lord Gosforde was intent on marrying her for her money.

She thought he was very old. At the same time, it would be impossible for any man, whatever his age, not to be attracted by anyone so lovely and unspoilt.

The Duke knew that Alysia would be shocked and perhaps terrified by the advances he would make to her.

The Duke had never had anything to do with young girls.

However, he was aware there were any number of men who deliberately liked despoiling virgins.

It did not matter whether they were of the servant class or their own.

He considered it appalling.

He thought, in any case, that a man who was brute enough to beat Alysia should in fact be shot.

They reached the village.

Just before they came to the first cottage the Duke saw a small copse of trees at the entrance of the Church-yard.

He thought that that, at any rate, was a good place to leave Alysia.

He told her to hide herself as best she could while he went into the village.

Alysia moved under the trees.

Then she said to him like a child:

"Y-you will . . . come back?"

"You must know I would not leave you," the Duke said firmly. "Now hide yourself, but not so that *I* cannot find you, or that will certainly delay our journey."

She looked up at him trustingly and said:

"I will be waiting for you."

The Duke walked towards the village.

When he reached it he looked back, but there was no sign of her.

He knew she was behind some bushes and it was very unlikely that anybody passing would search them.

The Village Inn was very like the one at which he had stayed last night.

The food, however, was slightly better.

He asked the Landlord to place some slices of ham, cheese, and a little salad on a few pieces of paper.

"It is such a nice day," he said, "so I want to have a picnic out in the fields and not feel constricted by walls and people."

The Landlord laughed.

"Ye must be one o' they smart young Gentlemen as comes from th' City," he said. "It be all roight in t'Summer, but they shivers in th' Winter an' all they wants be to sit as near t' th' foire as they c'n get."

"Well, there is no need for a fire to-day," the Duke replied. "What I would like is some of your best cider."

As this was sold by the mugful, he was wondering how he could carry some to Alysia.

Then he had an idea.

"I am thirsty after walking in this heat, and if you will let me take a jug of your cider with me, I swear to you I will bring the jug back. But in case you do not trust me, I will give you a florin as a security for it."

As a jugful would have cost less than a florin, the Landlord agreed.

Finally, the Duke left the Inn with the jug containing the cider. He carried the food on the plate, which he had also promised to return.

As he walked away he thought that Harry would have been proud of him for being able to improvise his comforts.

It was something he had never done before.

Alysia gave a cry of joy when he arrived.

They ate off the same plate and drank from the same jug.

"Now I am going to take it back," the Duke said when they had finished. "Then we will make a detour to avoid the village."

They had not taken long in eating, and they set off again.

Because it was very hot, the Duke removed his coat and carried it over his arm.

"Let me carry your bag," Alysia offered. "I suppose you realise I have brought nothing with me, and no money with which to buy anything."

She looked at him with large eyes, then said unexpectedly:

"Perhaps I . . . should go back . . . you know I will only be an . . . encumbrance to . . . you. And . . . wherever we go . . . people will think it . . . strange that I am . . . with you."

She blushed as she spoke.

The Duke was aware that it had only just occurred to her that he was a man she had never met until this morning.

Of course people would think there was something strange in their relationship.

Because he did not want her to be nervous or upset, the Duke said:

"I have already thought of that. You are my sister and we are travelling to our home in Berkshire, but unfortunately, we had an accident. The horse that was drawing us was injured while a wheel came off our carriage."

Alysia was listening wide-eyed, like a child who was being told a bed-time story.

"Because we found it boring to sit about doing nothing," the Duke continued, "we walked on. The carriage, as soon as it is repaired, and the horse, when it has been patched up, will follow us."

Alysia clasped her hands.

"You are clever! That is so plausible and I am sure everybody will believe it!"

"We will make certain they do," the Duke said as he smiled. "Now, as you know this part of the world, have you any idea where we can stay the night?"

"If we walk quickly," Alysia said, "I know there is a village about five miles from here where there is a very pretty Inn. I have never been inside it, but once they had a Meet of the foxhounds there which I attended with my Mother."

"I imagine you are a good rider," the Duke remarked.

"I love riding," Alysia said, "and it was fun when we rode together, but when Mama married my Stepfather it was . . . different."

She paused for a moment before she said:

"I think he always suspected I did not believe the flattering things he said to Mama. I sensed even at the very beginning there was something wrong about them."

"Do you mean he did not love your Mother?"

"I do not think he is capable of love," Alysia replied. "He would never take me riding with them, and so I had to go with a groom, but it was not the same."

"No, of course not," the Duke agreed.

He was thinking how lovely Alysia would look on one of his horses.

Then he told himself that it would be a very great mistake to become involved any more than he already was with this lovely young girl.

He would take her to his Grandmother.

He would contact his own Lawyers to see what could be done about her fortune.

After that, he need have nothing further to do with her.

He had the uncomfortable feeling that he was becoming more deeply involved.

It was something which he might easily regret later.

As far as he was concerned, somebody as young and beautiful as Alysia could play no part in his life.

She certainly did not fit into the same category as Lady Antonia, or, indeed, the position occupied by Cleone.

"My Grandmother will look after her," he told himself confidently, "but I really could not stand by and see her drown herself."

They walked on and, now that she was happy,

Alysia began to talk of the countryside.

She told him about its folklore, and the Duke found it extremely interesting.

She was obviously very intelligent.

While he had doubted that at first, he admitted now that it was no exaggeration.

They had almost reached the village of which she had spoken, when Alysia said unexpectedly:

"Theodore means 'The Gift of God,' and as you have brought me life, perhaps that is the greatest gift that anybody could give to another."

"That is true," the Duke agreed. "You must therefore be careful of what I have given you and never again take risks with it."

"I knew it was wrong . . . of course I knew that," Alysia said, "and I was . . . praying all the time that God would forgive me. Then, as I looked up to Heaven, you spoke and everything . . . changed."

She gave a little skip as she walked and said:

"I feel now as if the dark clouds that have been menacing me have gone away and I am happy as I used to be before Mama died."

"That is what you should always be," the Duke said in his deep voice.

There was another half-a-mile to go before they reached the village.

It was larger than the Duke had expected.

There were more cottages and an ancient grey stone Church.

The Inn on the edge of the village green was as attractive as Alysia had said it was.

They went inside, and the Duke saw a pleasant-looking man behind the Bar.

"Good-afternoon!" he said. "My sister and I are

hoping you can put us up for the night. We have walked a long way and are now very tired."

"Ye wants rooms for t'night!" the Inn-Keeper exclaimed. "That be a change, to be sure!"

The Duke raised his eye-brows.

"You do not have many visitors?"

"We ain't 'ad none here for nigh on three months," the Inn-Keeper said, "but Oi'll show ye where ye can sleep."

He paused to say:

"'Twill cost ye two shillin' th' night, an' Oi'll be glad if ye'll pay me in advance."

The Duke put a five-shilling piece down on the Bar.

"That is for our rooms and for breakfast," he said. "I will pay for a good dinner after I have had it, and as we are hungry, it must be a very good one!"

The Proprietor was obviously very happy at having visitors.

His wife was a worried-looking woman who had more lines on her face than she should have had at her age.

She went up the stairs in front of them.

They were shown into two rooms, sparsely furnished but spotlessly clean.

"We are delighted to have these," the Duke said, "and now before we wash for dinner my sister and I would be grateful for a cup of coffee, or tea, whichever is available."

"Oi thinks us've some coffee left," the woman said. "But things be a bit short, as no one comes 'ere for meals."

"Why is that?" the Duke asked curiously.

"They be strange people in these parts," the woman explained. "My man an' me come here to try and make a living, but somehow we be still strangers. Th' men would rather sit at 'ome than come to th' Bar, as we expected them to do when us comes here over a year ago."

She bustled away without saying any more.

When she had gone downstairs the Duke said:

"It sounds a sad story."

"People in the woodside were always suspicious of strangers," Alysia said. "Mama used to say that one could live and die in the English countryside before anyone realised you were there!"

"You did not have many friends?" the Duke asked.

There was silence before Alysia said:

"We had a few, but Papa and Mama preferred to be on their own. Then, after Mama married Miles Maulcroft, nobody came because they did not like him."

The way she spoke made the Duke realise that she had lived a very lonely life.

This was why she was so unselfconscious.

He could not imagine that any young woman who had been to London, or even taken part in the Country festivities, would not have been aware of her beauty.

She talked to him not as if he was an attractive man.

He might have been her Father or her Uncle, certainly not a handsome Duke.

He knew Harry would have been amused, and his eyes twinkled as he said:

"Are you telling me you have met no young men

to pay you compliments, especially when you were out hunting?"

"There are very few Gentlemen who ride in the pack to which we belong," Alysia said. "Anyway, Mama would not allow them to speak to me because we had not been introduced. When I went hunting once with my Stepfather, the Gentlemen there were obviously avoiding us."

The Duke thought her story became more and more unexpected and more strange with everything she told him.

He could not help finding it intriguing.

He wanted to know a great deal more about Alysia.

He had no wish to make her nervous, however, by asking her too many questions.

They drank the coffee, which was of the very cheapest variety.

They enjoyed some home-baked bread and a comb of honey.

Now there were quite a number of children playing outside on the green in front of them.

Unexpectedly Alysia said:

"Why do we not help these poor people? It must be very frustrating for them, living in this beautiful Inn and having no visitors except ourselves."

"What do you suggest we do?" the Duke asked.

"As we obviously cannot afford to give them money," Alysia said, "and I, as you know, have not a penny to my name at the moment, we must make money come to them."

"How do we do that?" the Duke enquired.

"I was just thinking . . . perhaps we can tell the villagers that something . . . interesting is going to happen here to-night."

She jumped up from where she was sitting on the wooden bench and ran inside.

The Duke waited, thinking she was certainly unpredictable.

She came back, saying:

"What do you think? The Proprietor says there is a man in the village who plays the violin and I am sure you can sing if he plays for you."

"Sing?" the Duke repeated in astonishment.

"I will dance," Alysia said, "and I can dance very well because Papa had me taught by the very best Dancing Teacher in the neighbourhood."

The Duke stared at her in astonishment.

Before he could say anything, Alysia ran towards the children who were still playing on the green.

"Listen to me," she said, "will you all go home and tell your parents and your neighbours that there is a special party at the Fox and Duck to-night at eight o'clock. Tell them to come and that it will be something quite new and very exciting."

"Can we come too?" one of the children asked.

"Of course you can! Bring all your friends."

The children ran off, and Alysia came back to the Duke.

As she reached him she undid her pearl necklace, took it from around her neck, and put it into his hand.

"I know that is valuable," she said, "because it belonged to Mama. I wish I had brought all her jewellery with me. But if you would be very kind and give me enough money to pay the Musician to-night, you can sell the necklace to pay yourself back."

The Duke was astonished.

He was so used to women expecting him to pay for everything.

He could hardly believe that Alysia was entrusting him with a valuable piece of jewellery in exchange for what he imagined would be a few shillings.

"I understand what you are trying to do," he said, "and I tell you what—I will contribute to it."

"How?" Alysia asked.

"I will tell you that when our guests arrive," he said, "but I think after this they will be a great deal more friendly with the Inn-Keeper and his wife than they are at the moment."

"I knew you would understand," Alysia said impulsively. "How clever and wonderful of you. I do not know how to thank you."

chapter four

THE Musician was playing a cheerful tune on his violin.

On Alysia's instructions, all the chairs had been taken outside the Inn.

The Inn-Keeper and his wife, bemused by what was happening, obeyed every instruction they were given.

This included spreading some coloured blankets on the ground.

"Those are for the children to sit on," Alysia said to the Duke.

He looked around at what was arranged and said:

"You must not be disappointed if no one comes."

"I am sure they will," Alysia replied confidently, "out of curiosity, if nothing else."

She smiled before she added:

"I can see you have never lived in a small village.

69

Everything that happens is known and talked about the minute it happens, otherwise they feel they have been deprived."

The Duke laughed.

"We will see whether you are right or wrong by the end of the evening."

He was, however, talking to the air.

Alysia had gone back into the Inn.

He knew she was helping Mrs. Parkinson, the Proprietor's wife, in the kitchen.

They were preparing small tit-bits that could be eaten without troubling about plates or knives and forks.

There were little squares of cheese, each decorated surprisingly with half a glacé cherry.

There was a mouthful of crispy bacon, small pieces of fish on slices of toast, and little tomatoes stuffed, which children love.

All was arranged on large plates decorated with lettuce from the garden.

Alysia was still working when the Duke came to the door to say:

"I think some of your guests are arriving!"

Alysia ran to wash her hands at the sink.

She took a perfunctory look at herself in the mirror which hung over it.

As she did so, the Duke, watching, wondered how many other beauties would be so casual about their appearance.

He said nothing as Alysia ran across the kitchen to where he stood in the doorway.

"You will . . . help me?" she begged in a low voice.

"I told you I would," he answered, "but this is your party and I am really just a guest."

"A very *important* guest," Alysia added firmly.

She was not speaking in the flirtatious manner that other women used.

She just stated it as a fact.

They went out of the Inn and Alysia saw that the children had arrived.

Behind them, coming slowly, were the adults.

They were walking as if they felt it would be a mistake to appear too eager.

They were mostly the Mothers of the children.

Alysia shook hands with them and invited them to sit on the chairs, where they could listen to the Musician.

The Duke waited until quite a number of the men had arrived.

They were laughing amongst themselves, as if they were scornful of what was intended.

At the same time, they were determined to see what was going on.

When the chairs were nearly full, the Duke rose to his feet and said:

"This party has been arranged by my sister because she felt that the Proprietors of this beautiful Inn, who are new to the village, are feeling lonely. We have therefore asked you here to-night to show that English people, wherever you may find them, always hold out the hand of friendship and give a newcomer a chance."

He could see the surprise on the faces of the audience at what he was saying.

"What has been arranged," he went on, "with Mr. and Mrs. Parkinson, is that there is one drink for everybody as a welcome toast which will cost you nothing. It is a present from me and the owners of the Fox and Duck."

There was a gasp at this, then one of the men remarked:

"That's good news!" and clapped his hands.

As if they felt they could do nothing else, everybody clapped too.

Then the Duke finished:

"And the second drink, which I know you will all want, you must pay for. Now, as you drink the first one, I want you to raise your glasses and wish Mr. and Mrs. Parkinson Good Luck and happiness now that they have come to live amongst you."

There was a little murmur at this.

Then the Proprietor and his wife came from the Inn carrying huge trays on which there were mugs of beer and cider, lemonade for the children, and a few glasses of port for the older men.

The Duke waited until everyone held a glass in his hand.

Then he raised his.

"To Mr. and Mrs. Parkinson!" he said. "And may God bless them and the Fox and Duck, and of course everyone else in this happy and delightful village!"

The guests all raised their glasses and shouted "Good Luck!"

Alysia, looking at Mr. and Mrs. Parkinson, realised they were smiling. Yet, at the same time, they were a little embarrassed.

They hurried back into the Inn.

Alysia moved to stand beside the Duke.

He held up his hand and the talking ceased.

"What my brother and I have planned," Alysia said in her sweet voice, "is that to amuse you, everybody will try and contribute some sort of 'Turn.' I am going to start off by dancing, and I hope some of the children will join me."

She had already arranged it with the Musician.

He broke into an attractive tune which she thought would be known to most people in the village.

Because she had danced ever since she was a small child, she was not upset by having an audience.

She moved onto the green grass and danced with a grace and a sense of rhythm which the Duke appreciated.

He thought, in the light of the setting sun which turned the sky to crimson, that she looked like a young Goddess who had come down from Olympus to bemuse mere mortals.

After she had danced for a few minutes, Alysia beckoned to the children.

Some of the smaller ones ran towards her.

She took their hands and they swung round to "Ring-a-Ring-o' Roses."

The older children then joined in and their Mothers sat watching them proudly.

When the music stopped, Alysia curtsied and the girls tried to follow her example, while the boys bowed.

There was a burst of applause.

The children sat down again on the blankets.

Alysia looked at the Duke.

He had already had a word with the Musician when he arrived.

He told him that the only song he knew well was "The Eton Boating Song."

As the man was gifted with his violin, he was able to play the tune after the Duke had hummed it to him.

Now in his baritone voice the Duke sang the song which was known to every Etonian.

His voice was deep and seemed to ring out over the green.

As he repeated the chorus, first the children, then the men joined in:

Row, row together
With our bodies between our knees . . .

He sang it three times, then, amid a roar of applause, went back to his seat.

Then there was quite a rush of people who wanted to show what they could do.

One boy could play a tune on a pipe he had carved himself.

Although it was not very good, he was obviously popular in the village.

The boys who were members of the choir sang two verses of a Carol they had learnt at Christmas.

The girls, not to be outdone, sang another which Alysia guessed they had performed in a Nativity Play.

At last it seemed that the talent was exhausted.

The older men, who had been drinking mug after mug of ale which they had paid for, sang a rollicking song that was known to them all.

The Duke had never heard it before, but he guessed it was sung wherever there was a party given in the village, or at an outing.

Suddenly he was thinking that this was the kind of thing that Harry would approve of him knowing.

The sun sank and, when it was almost too dark to

see any more, the Mothers began to take the smaller children home.

The men who were drinking moved inside to the Bar.

Nobody noticed when the Duke drew Alysia up the stairs.

"This is where we retire," he said. "Remember, we have a long walk in front of us to-morrow."

"It was a good party," Alysia said happily, "and I am sure after this Mr. and Mrs. Parkinson will not be lonely any more!"

"It was clever of you to think of it," the Duke said quietly.

They reached their bed-rooms and he remarked:

"By the way, as you have nothing to wear, I thought perhaps you would like to borrow one of my shirts."

"Are you quite sure you will not want it yourself?" Alysia asked.

"Quite certain!" the Duke replied.

"Of course, I will wash and press it when we reach the place to which you are taking me."

"You know how to wash a shirt?" the Duke asked.

He thought, as he spoke, it was something that would be completely unknown to any previous women of his acquaintance.

"Of course I do!" Alysia replied. "My Mother used to tell me how Mister Brummell had always maintained that a Gentleman's shirt should be allowed to whiten in the sun."

She glanced at the Duke before she went on:

"I am sure when you are in London your clothes are washed in that way on Hampstead Heath, where all the *Beaux* send theirs."

The Duke thought that, in the clothes Harry had

borrowed for him, no one could compare him to the *Beaux* of St. James's Street!

Aloud he said:

"I should be delighted if you would wash my shirt, but where we are going I think you will find there are sufficient servants to do it for you."

"It will be no hardship," Alysia said. "You have been so kind, so very, very kind, and there is so little I can do for you."

She turned her face up to his as she spoke.

The Duke had a sudden desire to kiss her.

She looked so lovely, and he was certain that she had in fact never been kissed by a man.

Then he told himself severely that once again he was getting involved.

Quickly he opened the door of his bed-room.

He had left his bag on a chair.

He opened it and drew out one of the white shirts which Harry had packed for him.

He handed it to Alysia.

"Put this on," he said, "and try to go to sleep as quickly as possible. I will wake you soon after seven."

She took the shirt from him, then she said:

"Thank you! Thank you for a lovely evening! It was so exciting that I forgot to be afraid. But anyway, I know I am . . . safe with . . . you."

She gave him a very sweet smile and went to her room.

The Duke stood still until he heard Alysia's door shut.

With a sigh he shut his own.

"She is not for me!" he said sharply, and started to undress.

Alysia was fast asleep when there was a knock on her door.

"It is seven o'clock!" she heard the Duke say.

She got up quickly.

By the time she was dressed she knew that the Duke had already gone downstairs.

She found his bag lying on his bed and carefully packed the shirt she had borrowed into it.

She knew he would not mind if she also borrowed his comb.

She arranged her hair in the mirror, wishing she had another gown to put on.

The one she was wearing still looked fresh and uncreased, but she thought of the many pretty gowns she had left at home.

She wondered if Mr. Field would admire her in them.

Then she told herself she must be careful not to make him regret his kindness in letting her accompany him.

It seemed strange that he was walking such a long distance and that he could not afford to hire a horse, even if he could not buy one.

He had enough money to buy everybody drinks last night.

Yet she was aware his coat was somewhat threadbare and so was his silk tie.

Perhaps, she contemplated, he had lost all his money in some way.

She thought it could not have been through gambling, for he seemed such a sensible person.

Her Father had always said:

"Only fools gamble at cards or with the counters because the odds eventually are always against them."

'I am sure Mr. Field is a very clever man,' Alysia told herself.

She did not quite know why, but she knew he was unmistakably a Gentleman of whom her Father would have approved.

He also spoke as if he was well-educated.

Her Father had described to her often enough how some men pretended to a knowledge they did not really possess.

It was only a veneer.

"They usually get away with it," he said, "but they do not deceive somebody like me, who has studied all my life and am aware how much there is still for me to learn."

Alysia had laughed.

"Papa, you know everything!"

"I wish that were true," he replied, "but at least I know enough to recognise a fraud, whether it concerns a man, a picture, or a piece of furniture."

Alysia had laughed at this and challenged him.

Whenever they went shopping in the Town they would look in the windows of the shops which had very expensive things to sell.

She would then make her Father tell her whether what they saw was a genuine masterpiece, or just a fraud.

He had been right every time, she discovered.

She thought now that her Father would have approved of Mr. Theo Field and would have been convinced that he was genuine.

She looked round, saw that he had left nothing in

the bed-room except for his bag.

She ran down the stairs with it.

The Duke was already in the Parlour eating his breakfast.

"Hurry!" he said. "Your breakfast is getting cold."

Alysia put the bag down on a chair.

"I found your comb," she said. "I hope you do not mind that I used it?"

The Duke smiled and made a gesture with his hand.

"In the words that are invariably used in the East: 'Everything I have is yours!' Unfortunately, there is very little of it!"

"Everything we want," Alysia said, "except perhaps for two outstanding horses."

"I agree with you," the Duke said, "but unfortunately those I cannot provide."

Alysia felt she had been a little tactless and said quickly:

"It is lovely to walk in the sunshine, and perhaps to-night we shall find another attractive Inn like this one, although I doubt it."

"I doubt it too," the Duke remarked.

They finished their breakfast and he picked up his bag.

He put the old-fashioned hat on his head.

"Are you ready?" he asked.

"We must say good-bye to the Parkinsons," Alysia said.

"Of course," he agreed.

They walked from the Parlour into the Bar, where the Proprietor was polishing the glasses.

The Duke put some money down on the counter, but Parkinson pushed it back towards him.

"After wot ye've done for me," he said, "th' least the Missus and Oi can give ye both is a bed for t'night."

The Duke, who had paid him before the party for the free drinks he had given to the villagers, said:

"If you feel like that, I can only thank you, and wish you the very best of luck in the future."

"Any luck Oi 'ave is due to ye an' yer pretty sister!" the Proprietor answered. "Take care o' yerselves. Oi feel ye shouldn't be walkin'."

"It is good for our health and strength," the Duke replied.

He shook the Proprietor by the hand.

His wife then appeared from the kitchen and kissed Alysia.

"Oi'll never forget what ye've done f'r us. Ye're an Angel from Heaven itself."

"I hope one day I shall be able to come back and see you," Alysia promised, "but I know by then that the place will be so crowded that you will be unable to fit me in."

"There'll always be a bed for ye!" Mr. Parkinson said. "An' God's blessing be on yer 'ead."

He turned away as if he was embarrassed by his own words, and Mrs. Parkinson wiped her eyes.

The Duke drew Alysia out into the sunshine.

As they walked across the green she kept turning back to wave to Mrs. Parkinson, who was watching them go.

"I am sure things will be better for them now," she said.

The Duke wondered, had he been alone, if he would have been aware of the Parkinsons' suffering.

He also wondered whether he would have thought of a solution, as Alysia had.

"She is a very remarkable young woman!" he told himself.

Deliberately he tried to concentrate on the way they were going.

They walked until midday, when they stopped at an Inn.

It had a large number of guests because a "Mill" was to take place that afternoon.

It was only a pugilistic contest between two villages, but the Inn was packed.

The Duke therefore had to use his most authoritative manner in order to obtain some food for himself and Alysia.

When they managed to get it, they ate quickly.

Then they hurried away from the noisy crowd of men who already seemed to have drunk too much.

"I am glad we are not staying there!" Alysia remarked as they walked on.

"So am I," the Duke replied. "If there is one thing I dislike, it is a crowd of oafs urging two other men to do what they are too cowardly to do themselves."

"Papa always said that boxing was dangerous because hitting a man on the head could injure his brain."

"I suppose that is true," the Duke agreed. "But most people do not worry about their brain. Are you concerned with yours?"

"Of course I am!" Alysia said. "I want to use mine and I want to feel when I die that I have done something useful in the world. That, of course, depends on my brain."

The Duke smiled a little mockingly.

Most women, he thought, would have said it depended on their beauty and their bodies.

"So what do you think," he asked aloud, "you may have to contribute to the world in which we live?"

"I suppose we all want to make it a happier place because we have passed through it," Alysia said after a long silence.

"And I expect you think you would be given ten marks out of ten for what you did yesterday evening," the Duke suggested.

"No, I think about . . . five, and you will get five," Alysia laughed, "or perhaps, because you were so generous, you would get six and I would get four."

There was silence.

Then she said in a different voice:

"It was wonderful of you to give all those people drinks. It started off the evening so well, but please, will you take it . . . out of what you . . . get for my . . . pearls?"

The Duke remembered he had put them in his coat pocket.

He stopped walking to take them out, saying:

"You will wear these round your neck, and I assure you I have not yet sunk to taking money from a woman!"

Alysia wanted to argue with him. Then she remembered her Stepfather.

Because she was embarrassed, the colour rose in her cheeks.

"I . . . I never thought . . . you would . . . do that," she said after a moment, "but I did not . . . want to feel I had . . . deprived you when it was my idea to entertain . . . the people from the . . . village."

The Duke put the pearls round her neck and fastened them at the back.

"I think this continual talk about money," he said, "would have offended your Father. Intelligent women know it is a subject that is not discussed by Ladies of Quality."

To the Duke's surprise, Alysia laughed.

"I am not a Lady of Quality," she said, "and money is something we will have to discuss sooner or later."

"Why?" the Duke asked.

"Because I am in your debt in several ways, and if I am to get hold of any of my money, I would rather give it to you than to people who have done nothing to deserve it."

"Very well," the Duke agreed briskly. "We will talk about money when, as you say, you can get hold of it. I have a feeling, however, it is not going to be easy."

Alysia sighed.

"That is what I think too, but in the meantime, I do not want to be a liability."

"That is something you are not!" the Duke said firmly. "And, quite frankly, I would have found this walk very dreary if you had not been with me."

Alysia gave one of her skips.

"When you say things like that," she said, "I no longer feel embarrassed with every mouthful I eat and the comfortable bed I sleep in."

"Anyone as pretty as you," the Duke said without thinking, "usually accepts that sort of thing as their right."

"Why?" Alysia asked.

He knew in her innocence she would not understand, and after a moment he replied:

"Come on! We are walking slowly because you are trying to use your brain. Put that tiresome object to which you attach so much store into your feet, because they are what matter at the moment."

"Y-yes . . . of course," Alysia agreed.

As she spoke, she glanced over her shoulder.

It was as if she expected to see her Stepfather looming up behind her.

The Duke put out his hand and took hers.

"I am only teasing," he said. "I am enjoying your brain as I am enjoying having you with me. And, as money is a subject that is barred, what shall we talk about?"

"You," Alysia said. "You have told me nothing about yourself."

"That is something I will do at the end of the journey," the Duke answered.

"Why not now?"

"Because it is a long and boring story," he replied, "and when I tell you about anything as important as *me*, I expect you to concentrate on every word!"

He was teasing her again, and Alysia laughed.

"You know I will do that," she said. "I think you are the most interesting person I have ever met and so, of course, I shall want to know everything about you."

"That is asking a great deal," the Duke protested.

"I am sure you have done many exciting things in your life," Alysia went on, "and, as I said, as you are so clever and so very much a personality, I find it difficult to understand why you have not earned enough to enable you to ride a horse."

The Duke thought this was one of the most twisted, and at the same time most sincere, compliments he had ever received.

"That is also something I will explain later," he said.

Alysia's fingers tightened on his.

"You know," she said in a low voice, "if it is ever possible for me to help you, I will do so."

"I have just told you," the Duke said, "that a man, if he is a man, cannot take money from a woman."

There was silence, and they walked on a little way before Alysia said:

"Papa had very little money compared to Mama, but because they loved each other it was . . . something which never . . . troubled them."

"Of course not," the Duke said. "When one is in love, anything is possible, but we were talking about ordinary men and women, which is a different thing."

"We all want to fall in love," Alysia argued. "Everybody needs love, but very often they are unlucky and do not . . . find it."

"I suppose love is what you want," the Duke said.

"Of course I do," Alysia replied. "I want the love that made Mama so happy. All she thought about was Papa, and he loved her so much that nothing else in the world was of any importance."

"Then they were both very fortunate," the Duke said.

As they walked on, he wondered if he would ever find the idyllic love which Alysia was seeking.

He thought that if she was disappointed, it might spoil something that was very precious.

It made her different from anyone else he had ever met.

He was quite certain that love, as she sought it, was a sacred emotion emanating from God.

She must not be hurt by anything worldly, cruel, or unpleasant.

In other words, it was a childish dream.

Nothing in real life could live up to her expectations.

"She will be disillusioned," the Duke told himself. "Of course she will! She will discover that the 'Dream Man' whom she is seeking is not a 'Knight in Shining Armour,' but just an ordinary being with human faults and failings."

It hurt him to think of Alysia crying because she was disappointed, perhaps becoming cynical and bitter like so many other people.

'She needs protecting and looking after,' his mind told him.

Then he shied away from the implications in that thought.

They walked a long way before the Duke was aware that they were in a desolate part of the Country.

There seemed to be a very long distance between the last village and the next, which was not even in sight.

He knew without her telling him that Alysia was growing tired.

He thought, although she had never complained, that her feet were sore.

"We will stay the night at the next village we come to," he said. "There is sure to be an Inn."

"It will not be as charming as the Fox and Duck,"

Alysia said, "but perhaps we may be lucky."

They reached the Inn in another twenty minutes.

Looking at it, the Duke thought it appeared adequate.

It was, however, obviously not in such good repair as the one they had just left.

There were a number of men sitting outside it, drinking ale and laughing loudly.

However, it was too late for them to go any farther.

The Duke himself was beginning to feel tired, and it was not surprising that Alysia was dragging her feet.

They went into the Inn.

The Proprietor was an elderly, tight-lipped man.

"I want two bed-rooms, one for myself and one for my sister," the Duke said.

The Proprietor gave Alysia a sharp glance.

It told the Duke without words that he suspected that if she was anyone's sister, she was not his.

"Oi've got two rooms," he answered, "but they ain't together."

The Duke frowned.

"It would be more pleasant for my sister to have her brother close to her."

"Tak' it or leave it," the Proprietor said. "We've a Steeple-Chase on termorrer an' we'll be full up afore nightfall."

"Very well, we will take them!" the Duke said quickly.

The Proprietor insisted on having his money before a slatternly woman took them up the stairs.

The first room was small but adequately furnished.

The second was at the far end of the passage with a window looking out onto the Mews at the back of the building.

The Duke thought this might be noisy and therefore said that was the one he would take.

"I . . . I wish I were . . . nearer to . . . you," Alysia murmured.

"It be on'y a step or two," the maid said in a somewhat disagreeable tone, "or ye could be together, if that be wot ye're wantin'."

"These two rooms will suit us," the Duke said sharply.

His tone made the maid flounce away with her head in the air.

The Duke took Alysia back to the first room which overlooked the front of the Inn.

He opened the door.

Then he realised what he had not noticed before, that there was no key in the lock.

"I think perhaps you would be less disturbed," he said, "if you used the other room."

"You need your sleep as much as I do," Alysia said.

"It takes a great deal to disturb me," the Duke replied.

He put his bag down, opened it, and took out the shirt Alysia had worn the night before.

"At least we are not . . . very far . . . apart," she said as if she were reassuring herself.

They went downstairs to have a meal.

The place was even more crowded than when they had entered it.

The men at the Bar were particularly noisy.

The Duke, however, managed to procure a table at

the far end of the Dining-Room.

They had to wait for a long time, but eventually they were brought something to eat.

The Duke was aware long before they had finished that Alysia was very quiet.

Finally, the cheese, which finished the meal, arrived.

Although the Duke was being very critical, it was quite edible.

"Now we will go upstairs," he said.

He took Alysia by the arm.

As they walked down the Dining-Room he was aware that the men present were all staring at her.

They had to pass by the Bar in order to reach the stairs.

There were suggestive remarks from those who were still drinking, and a roar of laughter followed them.

The Duke opened his bed-room door to see that everything was as he had left it, including his bag.

Then he walked along the passage to where Alysia was to sleep.

He looked out of the window and saw that the Stables seemed comparatively quiet.

He opened the window for her.

"This is the worst place we have found so far," he said, "and your bed looks lumpy."

"I think I could sleep on anything to-night," Alysia answered.

"Then hurry and get into bed," he said, "and do not forget to lock your door."

She looked at him in surprise before she asked:

"You do not . . . think that . . . anyone would . . . try and . . . come . . . in?"

"I think that lot downstairs have drunk too much to be able to remember where they are sleeping," he replied. "A pig-sty would be the right place for them!"

Alysia laughed.

"I see what you mean, and I will lock my door. But you will wake me when it is time to get up?"

"At seven o'clock," the Duke answered, "and let us hope we can get some breakfast quicker than we were served at dinner."

"I expect they are making a fortune," Alysia replied. "And we would so much rather the nice Parkinsons had it than them."

"Do not worry about anybody but yourself," the Duke said. "Good-night, Alysia."

She looked up at him, and put her hand on his arm, saying:

"Thank you for a . . . lovely day! It has been very exciting . . . being with . . . you. And every step we walk takes me . . . farther and . . . farther away from . . . my Stepfather."

"Forget about him!" the Duke said.

"I am . . . trying to. But I cannot help . . . knowing how . . . angry he will be that I have . . . escaped from . . . him."

There was a tremor in her voice that made the Duke want to put his arms around her consolingly.

Then he knew that this was another thing he must not do.

'The sooner we reach home, the better!' he thought angrily.

He walked to the door.

"Good-night, Alysia," he said. "Forget everything but that you are tired."

"I will try to, and thank . . . you . . . again," she said.

He went out into the passage and waited until he heard the key turn in the lock.

Then he walked away to his own room.

As he did so, he saw a pile of soiled sheets on the floor on the other side of the corridor.

It was obvious that whoever had used the room had now left, and the bed was being prepared for a newcomer.

He just glanced at the bundle, then he saw amongst the sheets, there was a newspaper.

He picked it up.

It was yesterday's *Morning Post*, obviously left behind by a guest who had come from London.

He picked it up and took it to his room, pulling off his coat as he did so.

There was a candle burning by the side of the bed.

It was not an expensive one such as those he used in his own house.

In order to read, therefore, the Duke sat on the edge of the bed, holding the newspaper as near to the candle as possible.

He had not read the news since he had left Brighton.

There was a political situation in which he was particularly interested.

Then he told himself that the only thing that mattered was that he should get Alysia to Eagle Hall as quickly as possible.

He then turned to the Sporting Page.

He read the names of the winners of the races which had been taking place since he had been "on the road."

Then he began to feel drowsy.

Without realising it, he moved to a more comfortable position against the pillows.

Before he had time to blow out the candle, he fell asleep.

chapter five

THE Duke awoke and saw that the sun was coming through the window.

He realised he had not undressed, but had fallen asleep on top of the bed.

He looked at his watch and saw that it was half-past-six.

This told him he had half-an-hour before he had to wake Alysia.

He therefore washed himself thoroughly in the cold water in the ewer on the wash-hand-stand.

He shaved and put on a clean shirt. He threw the one he had been wearing on the floor.

It was on Harry's advice, and he thought with a smile he would be amused that he had carried it out.

He brushed his hair and put on the second silk tie that Harry had packed in his bag.

It was, he thought, rather smarter than the bur-gundy-coloured one.

Then he walked down the passage to Alysia's room.

When he reached her door he lifted his hand to knock.

He then saw with a sense of shock that the lock had been broken and the door was ajar.

He pushed it open and found that the room was empty.

The bed had been slept in, and lying on the floor was the shirt which Alysia had borrowed to wear in bed.

For a moment he just stared round him.

Then he turned and ran down the stairs.

There was no sign of the Proprietor, but the maid, who had shown them to their bed-rooms, was sweeping the ashes out of the grate.

The Duke had great difficulty in keeping his voice low and calm as he asked:

"What has happened to the lady who was with me last night and whom you showed into the last room in the passage?"

"'Er be gone, Sir!"

"Gone? Where?" the Duke asked sharply. "Tell me what happened?"

The way he spoke now caused the maid to instinctively spring to her feet as if to defend herself.

"A Gent'man as said 'e were 'er Father comes for 'er very late."

"At exactly what time?" the Duke enquired.

"Must 'ave bin gettin' on for two o'clock," the maid replied. "There was 'bout three men as was still drinkin' in t'Bar, an' when 'e walks in 'e asks if a young lady's arrived with a man as 'ad no vehicle an' walked 'ere."

"Was he speaking to you?" the Duke asked.

"Aye, as t'Master were busy a-pouring out th' drinks."

"So you told him you thought it was the young lady who was sleeping upstairs."

"There wer'n't no other young ladies sleepin' 'ere last night," the maid said, "an' when Oi says 'er were pretty like, e says right away:

"'That's who Oi be looking for.'"

"So you took him upstairs?" the Duke asked.

"Why not?" the maid asked truculently, "when 'e pays Oi for doin' so."

"You might have told me he had arrived," the Duke suggested.

"Oi didn't know which room ye'd took," the maid retorted. "Oi peeped into yourn an' sees ye was asleep wi' th' candle still a-burnin'!"

"You did not think to wake me, but took the man to the other room."

"'E was 'er Father, wasn't 'e?" the maid asked angrily. "If ye'd run orf wi' 'er, ye could 'ardly 'spect 'im not to want 'er back."

With difficulty the Duke controlled his temper.

"The door was locked," he said. "He broke it open."

"It wer'n't very difficult," the maid said scornfully. "Oi've said over an' over agin them locks ain't much use."

"What happened after he had opened the door?" the Duke asked.

"'E goes in an' 'is daughter gives a scream afore 'e says:

"'Make one sound and I will kill the man who brought you here!'"

The Duke stiffened.

"You are quite certain that is what he said?"

"Oi were outside," the maid said. "Oi were a-waitin', in case they wanted me."

The Duke was aware that she had been eavesdropping because she wanted to know what was happening.

He then asked:

"Did he have a pistol with him?"

"Oi think so," the maid answered, "but 't were difficult t' see wi' only th' light of th' stars comin' through th' window. 'E 'ad somethin' in his 'and, for th' young woman says:

"'No! No! I'll come with you, but you must not hurt him. He has been kind to me.'"

"'You'll come with me at once!' 'Er Father says, 'Get dressed!'"

"So he let her get dressed," the Duke said as if he were committing everything the maid said to memory.

"'E stands at th' window lookin' out, an 'er were a-tremblin' as 'er puts on 'er clothes. 'E catches hold of 'er arm," the maid replied with relish, "an' says:

"'One sound out of you and that man 'as abducted you dies!'"

"'E didn't abduct me,' 'er says frightened-like, and 'e says: 'Shut up!' an' 'er never says 'nother word."

"What sort of carriage did they have?" the Duke asked.

"Ever so smart, it were," the maid replied. "Two 'orses, two men drivin' 'em—an' another man as was inside th' carriage, waitin' for 'em."

"Thank you," the Duke said. "You have told me what I wanted to know."

Then he gave the maid a guinea and hurried back upstairs to pick up his bag.

His brain was working quickly.

He came down again and, without speaking, he walked out through the back door into the Stables.

He went into the quite large Stable where there were five horses.

An Ostler was filling up their pails of water.

The Duke walked up to him with an air of authority.

"I want your help," he said, "and I will make it worth your while."

As he spoke he drew a sovereign from his pocket and allowed the man to see it as he held it on the palm of his hand.

He saw the glint of greed in the man's eyes before he said:

"'Ow can Oi 'elp ye, Sir?"

"I want to buy a horse," the Duke said, "and I want one urgently. Do you think these horses here are for sale?"

The Ostler scratched his head.

"Them 'orses be takin' part in th' Steeple-Chase. Their owners ain't as rich as all that, or they'd not be competin' for t' prize."

"How much is the prize?" the Duke asked.

"'Undred pound!" the Ostler said in a tone of awe.

"Let me look at the horses."

The Duke went from stall to stall.

The horses were in his opinion fairly rough except for one which he thought was considerably better than the others.

"Who does this one belong to?" he asked.

"Mister Turner, Sir. 'E be a young man as live

97

'bout six mile from 'ere.' 'E be stayin' th' night as 'e and 'is friends 'ad a party yes'day."

"I will speak to Mister Turner," the Duke said.

He gave the Ostler the sovereign and he grabbed it quickly.

"Thank ye, Sir, thank ye!" he said. "Oi'll 'elp ye any way Oi can."

The Duke, however, was already walking back into the Inn.

He found the maid alone in the Hall.

"Take me to the room occupied by Mister Turner," he said. "I expect you know who he is."

"Aye, Oi knows 'im right enough," the maid said. "Fancies 'isself, 'e does!"

She made no further comment, but walked ahead up the stairs.

Mister Turner, it appeared, was sleeping in the room almost opposite to the one the Duke had used.

He tried the door and, as it was unlocked, he pushed it open.

Mister Turner, who he thought was a man of about twenty-two or three, was fast asleep.

He looked as if he had imbibed rather heavily the night before.

The Duke shook his arm. But it took a few seconds to wake him.

"Hey, what is it?" he asked.

The Duke sat down beside the bed.

"I want to buy your horse!"

"What are you talking about?"

"I am telling you that I need a horse urgently. I have seen yours in the Stables and I will buy it from you and give you a great deal more than it is worth."

Mister Turner opened his eyes a little wider.

Then, as if he were finding it difficult to concentrate on what was being said, he asked:

"Did you say—did you really say you wanted to—buy my horse?"

"I want it now—at once," the Duke replied, "and if you will sell it to me, I will give you three-hundred pounds for it, which is far more than you would expect if you won the Steeple-Chase."

Mister Turner sat up in bed.

"I can understand you want my horse," he said, "but can you not wait until after the Steeple-Chase?"

"I want it now—at once!" the Duke repeated. "I am offering you three-hundred pounds for it."

Mister Turner stared at him as if he could not believe what he was hearing.

Because the Duke was impatient, he said:

"The answer must be 'yes' or 'no' immediately, otherwise I will buy one of the other horses in the Stable. I am sure one of those will be for sale."

As the young man did not answer, the Duke rose from the bed and went towards the door.

Before he could reach it, Mister Turner said:

"Here—wait! I've not refused your offer."

"And you have not accepted it," the Duke replied.

"I'll take it. I shall miss the Steeple-Chase, but . . ."

"It is a price you cannot refuse," the Duke finished.

He put his hand into his pocket and drew out a Note of Hand.

It was already signed.

As he was travelling under the name of "Field," if he had a large bill to pay, it would be a mistake for anyone to know his real name.

He put it down in front of Mister Turner and said:

"I must explain to you that I am buying this horse because I am the Manager of the Duke of Eaglefield's Stables, and have an appointment which I cannot miss in another part of the County. This Note of Hand is in the Duke's name, and as you are interested in racing, I expect you have heard of him."

"Of course I've heard of him," Mister Turner answered. "His horse won the Grand National Steeple-Chase this year, and I was there!"

"Then I know you will be pleased that, with the Duke, who loves horses, yours will find a good home."

The Duke looked round the room.

It was larger than the one he had used, and there was a desk at the far end.

He pulled it open and found there was an ink-pot and lying beside it was a quill.

"I will fill this in," he said to Mister Turner, "and you can cash it, as you will see, at Coutts' Bank or, if you pay it into your own Bank, they will obtain the money for you."

He pulled out a chair, sat down, and filled in the sum of three-hundred pounds.

Then he asked:

"What is your Christian name?"

"Simon," Turner answered.

The Duke filled in the Note, and waved it in his hand to help the ink to dry quickly.

Then, as he walked back to the bed, Simon Turner said:

"I suppose it's all right for me to let you have the horse! Supposing the Note of Hand's a dud? Then where will I be?"

The Duke stood facing him and now, slowly, he said:

"I understand you are a Man of the World, Mister Turner, and you will have met a lot of people racing and in other ways. I think you are experienced enough to know if a man is cheating you, as I should know if you were cheating me."

Simon Turner looked up at him.

As the eyes of the two men met, the Duke was exercising his willpower to get what he wanted.

He had dealt with quite a lot of men in his life, and he was not therefore surprised when Simon Turner succumbed.

"All right," he said, "I expect I can trust you."

"I assure you, on my Word of Honour, that you can," the Duke answered. "And as I wish to ride your horse, I need your saddle and bridle, so here is ten pounds in cash to pay for them."

He put the money down on the bed.

Then, before Simon Turner could say anything else, he added:

"Thank you very much, and should you run into any unexpected difficulties, you will find me at the Duke's house, Eagle Hall, in Berkshire."

He did not wait for a reply, but ran down the stairs and back to the Stable.

The Ostler helped him to saddle the horse and was appropriately gratified when he received a half-sovereign for doing so.

He led the horse from the Stable as the Duke went back inside the Inn.

He remembered he had not paid what was owing for dinner and for their rooms.

He put several notes down on the Bar and was

just leaving when the Proprietor, looking bleary-eyed and unshaven, came from the kitchen.

"What's goin' on?" he asked. "Oi 'ears from Emma ye've bin buying a 'orse."

"I have bought one," the Duke said briefly, "and I have left the money I owe you on the Bar."

"'Ow d'ye know how much ye owe?" the Proprietor asked suspiciously.

"I guessed what was correct and magnified it," the Duke replied. "I do not think you will be disappointed."

He went outside and swung himself into the saddle.

"Good luck, Sir!" the Ostler shouted as he rode off.

The Duke had never been mistaken in knowing if a horse was good or bad.

He realised the one he had just bought, while not exceptional like his own, was young and spirited.

He galloped him across the fields to start with, then settled down to ride at a sharp pace.

It was what his mount would be able to keep up all day without getting over-tired.

As he went he was planning exactly what he must do in order to save Alysia.

It never struck him for one moment that he might do nothing.

He was only furious that because they had not had rooms next to each other he had been unable to hear her leave.

Now he knew they had been foolhardy in drawing attention to themselves by trying to help the Parkinsons at the Fox and Duck.

He had also underestimated Miles Maulcroft's determination to get his Stepdaughter back.

Thinking over what he himself would have done in the circumstances, he thought the man had doubtless sent out grooms in every direction.

His own inquiries had led him to the Fox and Duck.

It was natural that the Parkinsons would have related how kind the pretty girl and the man she called her brother had been in helping them.

Miles Maulcroft would have realised that as they were walking, they would not be very far away.

As the Duke remembered, there had been no Inns later in the day before they reached the one at which Maulcroft found them.

He cursed himself for being a fool.

He should have guessed that a man who could murder his wife for her money was not likely to let his Stepdaughter get away easily.

"It is my fault," the Duke told himself, "and I have to rescue her."

As he rode on, he went over everything that Alysia had told him about her home.

It took him some time to recall that she had said the name of the village in which they lived.

It was when they were talking about the Parkinsons being lonely.

"It was just the same in Meadowley," she said.

That was the name of her village!

He expected he would find it on the map he had with him.

He was frightened of only one thing.

In his desire to make sure Alysia could not escape him again, her Stepfather would insist on her marrying Lord Gosforde immediately.

That, at least, the Duke tried to console himself,

would not be until to-morrow.

The way he had walked with Alysia had been straight across Country.

It was the way he was going back to find her.

But Miles Maulcroft would be obliged in his carriage to keep to the winding, twisting lanes.

It was impossible to go fast along them.

There were highways, but they mostly led directly to Brighton or to the other large towns in Sussex.

'I have to save her, not only from her Stepfather, but also from Gosforde,' the Duke told himself as he rode on.

He was well aware that it was not going to be easy.

He would have to use what Alysia valued so highly—his brain.

He had eaten no breakfast and he therefore stopped for a short time at about midday.

He was aware that he could have gone to the Fox and Duck, but he passed it by this time.

In any case, had no intention of going in to gossip with the Parkinsons.

It would certainly delay him.

Instead, he rode on.

Only when, late in the afternoon, his horse was beginning to tire a little did he leave the fields.

In a quarter of an hour he found a main road.

It was quite a busy one, and it was not surprising that there was a large Posting-Inn about a mile after he joined it.

The Duke rode into the court-yard and handed his horse over to an Ostler.

He then went into the Inn.

It was large and well-furnished.

The Proprietor greeted him in a suave manner

which told him he was used to dealing with important travellers.

"What can Oi do for ye, Sir?" he asked.

The Duke was aware that, as he spoke, the proprietor's eyes were taking in his somewhat worn coat.

He was not in any way as smartly dressed as a Gentleman would be.

"I want to speak to you on a very important matter," the Duke said, "and I would be grateful if we could go somewhere where we will not be disturbed."

The Proprietor looked somewhat surprised.

But he opened the door of a small room which was obviously where he did the accounts.

The Duke sat down and said:

"I am the Manager of one of the Duke of Eaglefield's Estates and I have just received instructions that I have to take a parcel of some value to His Grace at Eagle Hall, where I expect you know he lives."

"Oi've 'eard of His Grace," the Proprietor agreed.

"Most people have," the Duke replied, "if they attend Race Meetings."

"He's got some fine horseflesh," the Proprietor acknowledged.

"He has indeed," the Duke answered, "and I am riding one of them now."

He saw that the Proprietor was looking at him curiously while waiting to hear what he required.

"What I want from you," he said, "so that I can take this valuable parcel back to Eagle Hall, is a light carriage drawn by two of your best and fastest horses. As I am in a hurry to get there, they must be good."

The Proprietor made no comment, and the Duke continued:

"I will leave the horse I am riding now here in your keeping. It will, of course, be collected by a groom as soon as possible. As there will be a man waiting with the parcel when I pick it up, there will be no need for you to send a driver with me."

He paused as if he was feeling for words.

"I will drive the horses myself and I would prefer, as it would be lighter, either a small Chaise, or a Chariot, whichever is available, and which holds only two people."

"I understands," the Proprietor said.

"Now that you know my requirements, I hope you can provide what I am asking."

There was only a slight pause before the Proprietor answered.

"It's something I'd wish to do, and, of course, I'm pleased to have the patronage of His Grace. At the same time, you'll understand, Sir, that it'll be somewhat expensive."

"Of course, of course!" the Duke said in a lofty tone. "But money is no object. What is important is that His Grace does not like to be kept waiting and the parcel is needed immediately."

He drew from his pocket another of his Notes of Hand.

He made sure that the Proprietor saw that he had also a number of large notes.

"Here is a Note of Hand on His Grace's Bank, which is Coutts'," he said, "and I can also give you a small amount of cash, although I do not wish to be left too short on the return journey."

The Proprietor looked suitably impressed.

"His Grace's Note of Hand'll be quite sufficient, Sir," he said, "and I assure you we'll take the greatest care of the horse until it's collected."

"I knew I could trust you," the Duke said. "And now I would be obliged if I could wash and have something substantial to eat before I go on my way."

He was taken up to a very pleasant bed-room.

A can of hot water was provided for him, and having washed, the Duke studied his map.

He decided that by now he was only about three miles away from Meadowley.

He went downstairs to find a meal waiting for him, but he did not linger over it.

He knew it was important to find his way to Alysia before it grew dark.

The Proprietor had provided him with two fresh horses to draw the Chaise.

It had a hood which could be let down over the driver if the weather was bad.

It was certainly the best the Inn-Keeper could provide.

The horses being fresh, the Duke had some difficulty in keeping them under control, which pleased him.

He soon went from the main road back onto the narrow lanes.

It was impossible to go fast, even though he was in a hurry.

It took him some time to reach Meadowley.

When he had done so, he stopped the first child he saw.

He chose a child, knowing children were less likely to gossip or question who he might be than a man or a woman.

"Can you tell me the name of Mr. Maulcroft's house?" he asked.

The child, who was a boy of about ten, pointed down the road ahead.

"Turn right," he said. "Th' gates be by a wood."

The Duke threw him a couple of pennies which he caught with delight.

Then he drove on.

Now he went slower, not wishing to be noticed.

He was relieved to find that the wood was quite large.

The drive to the house also had an avenue of trees.

There was only one Lodge, but the iron gates were open.

He drove through them without, he hoped, being noticed.

Then, as he first saw the house ahead of him, he drew in his horses.

It was an attractive building and just, he thought, the sort of house he would expect Alysia to live in.

Long and low, it was obviously Elizabethan.

The setting sun turned the red bricks with which it was built to a soft shade of pink.

He could see even from this distance that the house was surrounded by a garden which was filled with colour.

The trees as well as the bushes were in bloom.

It flashed through his mind that it was a perfect setting for love.

That was why Alysia's Mother and Father had been so happy there.

Then he remembered the evil Demon who was now in control.

He turned his horses and, driving them into the

wood, travelled along a track until he reached a field on the other side.

The ground was hard because there had been no rain.

He continued along the field until he was parallel with the house.

By this time all the labourers would have returned to their homes.

There was not a sign of anyone, either in the fields or the woods.

The Duke drew his horses to a standstill, then attached them to a fence so that they could not escape.

They put their heads down and quite contentedly started to crop the grass.

The Duke walked into the wood.

He crept through the bushes beyond it, nearer and nearer to the house.

When he reached it, everything seemed to be very quiet.

There was no one in the garden, nor, as far as he could make out, in the house itself.

He was suddenly worried.

Perhaps instead of taking Alysia home her Stepfather had taken her to the house of Lord Gosforde.

She had told him it was not far away.

If that was so, then she might be married there before he could rescue her.

He moved a little nearer still to the house, wondering if he could look through the windows.

Then suddenly the front-door was opened and a man came out to stand on the steps.

The Duke had only one look at him and was sure it was Miles Maulcroft.

He was a good-looking man.

Yet his face was hard and cruel and there was something unpleasant about him.

The Duke could understand why Alysia had said she hated him from the first moment she saw him.

But he could also understand that in his own way Miles Maulcroft would be attractive to women.

He stood there on the steps, looking around him.

It was as if he were taking stock of what he owned, or what he intended to have.

After four or five minutes he turned back into the house, leaving the door open.

The Duke had learned what he wanted to know.

If Maulcroft was there, then Alysia was somewhere in the house.

He had thought a dozen times when he was riding here of what she had said and how she had escaped.

"There is a balcony to my bed-room," she had explained, "and I managed to tie a sheet to it and climb down it. It was difficult . . . but I was desperate!"

The Duke now went back into the wood and, making a detour, came towards the back of the house.

He realised how Alysia had originally escaped.

There were two balconies which over-looked the Rose-Garden, and beyond that was a Bowling-Green.

They must have been added at a much later period than when the house was built.

Because the ceilings of an ancient Elizabethan house were low, the balconies were not very high from the ground.

The Duke could therefore understand how, by

sliding down the sheet, Alysia had only a short drop to the ground.

He was wondering which balcony was hers.

Then, as the sun sank and dusk fell, there was a light in one of the windows with a balcony, but not in the other.

He had found out what he wanted to know.

It was always a mistake to linger unless it was absolutely necessary.

He therefore went back to his horses.

chapter six

THE Duke waited until it was nearly midnight.

It was difficult for him to be patient, but he sat in the Chaise and tried to relax.

He knew of old that before he was riding in a race or a Steeple-Chase it was always wise to relax his body, also not to feel agitated in any way.

He was well aware of the hazards that lay ahead of him in rescuing Alysia.

He thought she was in the room above the balcony.

At the same time, she might not be there.

If he had to search the house, there was every chance that somebody would see him.

He would then be in the uncomfortable position of an intruder.

If Miles Maulcroft had told Alysia that he would kill him, then he would not hesitate to do so if he found him wandering about the house.

He was, in fact, taking his life in his hands.

But because the position was dangerous and different from what he had ever done before, he had never felt stronger or more alert, or, if the truth was told, more interested and intrigued.

He was determined to rescue Alysia whatever the danger.

Every nerve in his body was ready to meet the challenge.

At last, when the moon was high in the sky and the stars were like diamonds, he thought the time had come.

He moved the horses even farther up the field.

Now he had only to walk in through the shrubs to reach the back of the house.

He tied the horses to a fence so that they would not stray.

Then he walked very quietly through the shrubs, taking no chances that he might be seen.

He made a detour so as not to cross the unshadowed lawn to reach the house.

He came alongside it to where he had seen a wooden seat.

It was heavy.

However, he managed because he was strong.

By lifting and pulling it over the soft grass, he put it immediately beside the wall under the balcony.

He took off his coat and shoes.

Climbing onto the back of the seat, he found he could touch the balcony.

Because he was extremely athletic, he pulled himself up and put his leg over the balustrade.

He had expected to find the window closed so that

Alysia would not be able to escape as she had done before.

To his surprise, however, it was open.

Very cautiously he stepped over the sill and into the room.

The moonlight was streaming in to illuminate part of the room.

It made a pattern of silver on the floor.

Beyond it the Duke could see the bed with somebody asleep in it.

Moving on tip-toe, he went nearer.

He knew that if it was not Alysia, he might have to make a very hasty retreat.

As his eyes grew accustomed to the darkness, he saw her hair spread out on the pillow.

He moved quickly to sit down on the side of the bed.

He bent forward, meaning to whisper in her ear.

At that moment she opened her eyes and looked up at him.

He thought she was about to give a scream either of horror or perhaps delight.

He bent lower still, and his lips were on hers.

As he touched them, he knew they were just as he had expected they would be—soft, sweet, and very innocent.

At first she stiffened, then her arms went round his neck.

It was then he knew that something very strange had happened.

The blood was throbbing in his temples.

Because her lips were beneath his, he felt a sudden ecstasy that was different from anything he had ever known before.

He realised in that second that surprisingly, incredibly, he had fallen in love.

He kissed her until he felt her move even closer to him.

Then he raised his head.

"You . . . have . . . come! You . . . have . . . come!" she murmured.

He could hardly hear the words, but he was aware of the rapture in them.

"I am taking you away," he whispered, "but do not speak, as it is dangerous."

It was then he felt her arms tighten.

As he held her a little closer, he was aware that she was naked.

Even before she said the words, he knew what she was about to say.

"He . . . has . . . taken . . . all my clothes away . . . so that I . . . cannot . . . escape."

The Duke raised himself.

In the far corner of the room he could see there was a wash-hand-stand.

He went towards it and found, as he expected, two linen hand-towels.

He picked them up and brought them back to the bed.

Then, bending, he said as Alysia's hair touched his mouth:

"Put these around you for the moment. I will not look while you get out of bed."

There was just a second while she questioned what he was doing.

Then she obeyed him.

He turned his back while she did so, knowing that he must not frighten her.

There was too much at stake.

She rose from the bed and moved to a corner of the room where the moonlight did not penetrate.

The Duke pulled off the bed-cover, which had been rolled back, then the blankets and sheets.

He carried them out through the window onto the balcony.

On the opposite side from where he had climbed he knew there was a flower bed.

First he flung down the bed-cover, pulling it out as wide as he could.

Then he dropped the two blankets on it and finally the sheets.

He went back into the bed-room and collected from the bed the bolster and two pillows.

As he took them towards the balcony, he was aware that Alysia was following him.

She had knotted one of the hand-towels round her waist.

The other was draped over her shoulders, concealing her breasts.

The Duke flung the two pillows and the bolster down on top of the bed-clothes.

Then, as he straightened himself, he found Alysia behind him.

He thought few women he had known in the past would have been intelligent enough to realise what he was doing.

She looked very lovely in the moonlight.

He longed to take her in his arms and kiss her.

But every minute, every second, was urgent, and it would be madness to linger.

He turned Alysia round so that she faced the garden.

Then he lifted her onto the balustrade of the balcony.

He wanted to tell her not to be frightened, but knew it would be a mistake.

Voices carried more penetratingly in the dark than anything else.

Instead, he grasped her by the wrists, and she knew exactly what he was going to do.

Very carefully he lowered her over the edge of the balcony.

Then he bent forward as far as was possible.

He steadied her until she was directly above the pillows he had thrown down.

Just for a second he held her suspended so that she could see what was going to happen.

Then he released her.

The only danger was that she might hurt herself and scream, or break a leg as she fell.

But she landed exactly as he had intended, on the pillows and the bolster.

He waited to see her sit up, unharmed.

Then he rushed to the other side of the balcony and scrambled down the way he had climbed up.

He put on his coat and shoes which he had left on the wooden seat.

Moving Alysia, who was standing waiting for him, to one side, he picked up the bed-clothes.

He kicked aside the pillows and wrapped her first in a sheet, then in one of the blankets.

He picked her up and, to her surprise, set her down on the wooden seat.

Then he placed the second blanket and the satin bed-cover in her arms before he picked her up again.

She was a bulky burden with all the bed-clothes.

At the same time, she herself was very light.

The Duke carried her swiftly across the lawn and into the shadow of the trees.

He was praying as he did so that nobody was watching them from the windows.

It took him only a minute or two to make his way through the shrubs.

The carriage and the horses were waiting.

He put Alysia down on the seat and covered her with the blankets and the bed-cover.

Then he released the horses.

He climbed in beside Alysia, picked up the reins, and drove off.

It had all taken a very short time.

It would have been impossible for anybody who had seen them on the lawn to have run downstairs and reached them.

The horses moved quickly across the fields.

The Duke remembered to turn in through the wood which brought them to the drive.

A few minutes more and they were moving swiftly through the village and along the lanes which led to the main road.

Only when they were quite some distance from Meadowley did the Duke speak for the first time:

"Are you warm enough?" he asked.

"I am ... dreaming ... I know I am ... dreaming!" Alysia replied. "How can you have ... been so ... wonderful, so ... marvellous as to ... find me?"

There was a little sob in her voice before she added:

"I ... I thought ... I was lost ... and my ... Stepfather has ... arranged for me to be ... m-married ... to-morrow."

119

The Duke turned his head for a moment to look at her.

Her eyes were shining as if the stars had fallen into them.

She looked so lovely in the moonlight.

He could not prevent himself from bending forward so that his lips touched hers.

Then, as he looked again at the road ahead of him, Alysia said:

"I . . . love you! How can I help but love you!"

"And I love you!" the Duke said quietly.

She gave a little gasp.

"Do you . . . mean it . . . do you really . . . mean it?"

"I will prove how much when we are not obliged to travel so quickly, as we are now," he answered.

He saw the little shudder that went through Alysia's body.

"Y-you do not . . . think that my Stepfather will . . . catch . . . up with . . . us?"

"I expect he will try," the Duke replied, "and that is why you have to be very brave and sensible. We have a long drive in front of us."

"I do . . . not mind . . . anything as . . . long as I can be . . . with you," Alysia said. "How did . . . you get these . . . horses and this . . . carriage?"

"I hired them," the Duke answered. "They are fresh and I think your Stepfather will find it difficult this time to take you back."

"I . . . I thought . . . when you found me gone," Alysia murmured, "you would not . . . trouble about . . . me any more and I was . . . doomed to . . . marry that . . . frightening man."

"How could you think I would be so cruel?"

the Duke asked. "Besides, it is a challenge, and so far we have been very lucky. But I am taking no chances."

"I realized when Step-Papa . . . burst into the room at the Inn . . . breaking the . . . lock," Alysia said, "that you . . . were too far away . . . from me to . . . hear what was . . . happening."

"I was crazy to have taken such a risk," the Duke said, "and even more foolish to have allowed you to help the Parkinsons at the Fox and Duck."

"My Stepfather told me that they said how . . . kind we had . . . both been and of . . . course he was . . . curious to know . . . who you were and . . . how you had . . . met me."

"What did you tell him?" the Duke enquired.

"I told him . . . nothing," Alysia said, "although he . . . hit me because I . . . refused."

The Duke frowned and his lips set in a hard line.

If he ever had the chance, he would make Miles Maulcroft sorry that he had ever hit anyone so small and vulnerable as Alysia.

She moved a little closer to him as she said:

"Step-Papa . . . threatened me that . . . if he could . . . find you, or you ever . . . came near . . . me again, he would have . . . you arrested for the . . . abduction of a minor."

"So that I would be transported?" the Duke remarked.

"D-did you . . . know that was . . . the penalty?"

"Of course I knew it!"

"And you . . . still came . . . to save . . . me! How can . . . you be so . . . kind and so . . . very . . . very . . . brave!"

"How could I lose anyone I love?" the Duke asked.

As he spoke, he knew that while he had not admitted it to himself, he had known long before he kissed Alysia that he loved her.

He had never had much to do with girls before.

He thought the *débutantes* he had seen in London were gauche and unattractive.

He had spent all his time with worldly, sophisticated married women.

They had brought flirtation to a fine Art.

They managed to be seductive with every word they spoke and every movement they made.

To him Alysia had seemed like the Spirit of Spring.

Completely unselfconscious, she brought a childlike enthusiasm and excitement to everything she said and everything she did.

At the same time, she was a woman.

He had been amazed at her beauty.

The loveliness of body bewitched him.

When he had let her down from the balcony onto the pillows below, the hand-towel she had placed over her shoulders had slipped away.

He had looked down to see that she was naked to the waist.

He thought in the moonlight she was like an Angel come down from Heaven.

He had only been able to look at her for a passing second.

Then he had crossed the balcony to climb down and join her.

He knew, however, that it was a picture that would remain in his mind for the rest of his life.

She was, in fact, the most beautiful thing he had ever seen.

He knew now that Alysia had brought him what

until now he had always missed.

It was real love that steeped through his veins, love which made the whole world a different place from what it had been before.

They drove on.

When the Duke reached the main road he gave the horses their heads.

There was no traffic.

The moon was so bright that there was no danger in travelling fast.

He had not lit the carriage lamps.

It had been too dangerous to do so while the horses were hidden beside the wood.

Now, for the moment, he wanted to put as many miles as possible between them and Miles Maulcroft.

The Duke knew it would be a mistake to under-estimate for a second time the resources of the man.

He had been caught out once, and he was ashamed of himself that it should have happened.

Now the only thing that mattered was to reach Eagle Hall, where he knew Alysia would be safe, at any rate, until Miles Maulcroft was aware of his identity.

They drove on and, after some time, the Duke asked the same question:

"Are you warm enough?"

"I am too . . . happy to be . . . anything . . . else," Alysia answered, "only my feet are a . . . little chilly."

The Duke picked up his bag from the floor of the carriage where he had put it before he left the Posting-Inn.

"You will find a pair of my stockings in the bag,"

he said. "Perhaps you could manage to put them on without my having to stop."

Alysia laughed.

"You think of . . . everything," she said. "How could I . . . imagine that . . . you could provide . . . me with stockings . . . if nothing else?"

The Duke thought she would have to thank Harry for that.

Alysia moved the blankets and the sheets carefully.

By lifting her feet one by one she managed to put on the clean stockings that had been in the bag.

They were too big for her, but they were warm and comfortable.

She leaned back once more.

The Duke pulled the bed-cover over her again while he drove with one hand.

"That is much better!" Alysia exclaimed. "But I am just wondering how you will provide me with clothes. I can hardly walk about . . . wherever we are going in just a . . . pair of your . . . stockings!"

She made it sound like a joke, and the Duke laughed again.

"I am going to wave my magic wand," he said, "and you will find yourself dressed like 'Cinderella' and undoubtedly the Belle of the Ball."

"'Cinderella' at least had some rags to wear!" Alysia said.

Then in a tone of consternation she exclaimed:

"I have just . . . realized that I am not wearing my pearls as I was when I was . . . with you before! Now I have nothing . . . nothing at all . . . of my own!"

"I can provide everything you want," the Duke said quietly.

"I am sure you cannot . . . afford it," Alysia

answered, "any more than . . . you can . . . afford this . . . carriage and horses with which you . . . saved me."

She paused before she added:

"Oh, please, Theo . . . was it very . . . wrong of me to . . . come away with you? I cannot imagine how . . . we can ever get . . . hold of my . . . money without letting my . . . Stepfather know . . . where I . . . am."

"I think you are being rather uncomplimenta-ry!"the Duke complained. "You did not trust me to come and save you, and yet I managed to spirit you out of your bed-room. You are already a long distance away from your Stepfather. Surely, after that you can trust me to provide you with clothes, food, and, of course, anything else you need?"

"All I . . . really need," Alysia said in a low voice, "is that . . . you should . . . love me . . . but I have to . . . think of . . . you and I . . . cannot allow you to . . . suffer or be in . . . difficulties because . . . of me."

The Duke thought this had never worried any of the women he had known in the past, and he answered:

"You must promise to trust me because I want everything that happens to be a surprise—a very pleasant surprise! So I am just going to tell you to— wait and see."

"I will do that . . . of course I will . . . do that," Alysia replied. "But I cannot . . . think how I can ever . . . thank you."

"I will tell you how to do that later on," the Duke answered.

She put her cheek for a moment against his arm.

125

It sent a thrill through him which again was different from anything he had felt in the past.

"I love her," he told himself, "and I will kill anyone who tries to take her from me!"

They drove on.

He thought after a little while that Alysia had fallen asleep.

It was not surprising that she should be tired.

She had spent last night travelling home with her Stepfather, while he had slept peacefully.

"It is the best thing she can do," he decided.

On and on the Duke went, driving with an expertise to which the horses responded.

They therefore covered many more miles than he had dared to hope for.

Finally, he felt they had travelled far enough and it was time to change to fresher horseflesh.

He drew into the yard of a large Posting-Inn which was on the main road to Reading.

They were now only about seven miles from Eagle Hall, but he thought it would be a mistake to push his horses any further.

It was still not yet three o'clock.

The Inn was silent although there were a number of Phaetons and Curricles parked in the court-yard.

After a minute or so the Night Ostler came from the Stables.

The Duke climbed out of the carriage, aware that because they had stopped Alysia had woken up.

"Evenin', Sor," the Ostler said. "Wot can Oi'do fer ye?"

"I want two of your very best horses," the Duke replied, "and I want them put between the shafts as quickly as possible."

The Ostler looked at him as if he were wondering what he was prepared to pay.

The Duke drew him to one side as if he did not wish Alysia to hear what he had to say.

"There is a Lady in the Carriage," he said in a low voice, "who is extremely ill. I am taking her to Eagle Hall, where she is to be the guest of the Duke of Eaglefield."

The Ostler made a murmur, and the Duke went on:

"I require two of your best horses to convey her for the rest of the journey. They will be returned to you the day after to-morrow. I want you to look after these two, as they belong to somebody from whom I have borrowed them and must be returned safely."

The Ostler nodded as the Duke continued:

"I will pay you well for obliging me, and I know His Grace will be grateful for your attention."

The words had a magic effect because, as the Duke knew, his name would be well-known in this part of the County.

The Ostler took him to where the Posting horses were kept.

The Duke chose two that he thought were the best and learned that they had not been taken out for three days.

He helped the Ostler take out the horses he had driven from between the shafts.

As they were put into stalls, the Duke said:

"Look after these animals well. They have come a long way and at great speed. I feel sure you will not fail me."

"Oi'll not do that, Sir," the Ostler replied.

The Duke helped him put the fresh horses between the shafts.

When the man was adjusting their bridles he went into the Inn.

As he expected, there was a night-porter in the Hall.

He was actually pouring himself out a cup of coffee.

The Duke picked it up, added sugar, saying as he did so:

"I require this for the Lady in the carriage outside who is too ill to move, and I would like for myself a glass of your best French brandy."

The night-porter, who realised he was richer than he looked, hurried to find the brandy.

The Duke carried the cup of coffee out to Alysia.

"I thought this was what you would like," he said. "Are you hungry?"

Alysia shook her head.

"No. My Stepfather sent me up some food while I was locked in my bed-room, and I ate a little of it."

"That was sensible of you," the Duke remarked.

She drank the coffee and smiled at him before he took the cup back into the Inn.

The night-porter had found a bottle of brandy.

It was undoubtedly French and of such a good vintage that the Duke suspected that Customs Duty had not been paid on it.

He was aware that the smugglers were still travelling between France and England, as they had done in the war.

Despite every effort by the Coast Guards to prevent them from doing so, they got their goods through.

He drank the brandy and put two sovereigns down on the table.

The night-porter pocketed them eagerly.

The Duke went out to find that the horses were ready and the Ostler was waiting for him.

The Duke put his hand into his pocket.

"I am going to pay you the usual charge for the hire of two horses," he said to the Ostler. "The rest is to be quite certain the other horses will not be used until they are fetched by His Grace's groom. It is also for your help and assistance, for which I am very grateful."

The man gasped as he saw the note which the Duke gave him.

He touched his forelock respectfully as the Duke got into the carriage, and picked up the reins.

The new horses were, as the Ostler had said, fresh.

The Duke drove them at the greatest speed of which they were capable for the last part of the journey.

He was eager to get Alysia to Eagle Hall and set the wheels in motion which would protect her from her Stepfather.

He thought it would be difficult for Miles Maulcroft to find her.

Yet they had been unlucky before.

The Duke was well aware that there would be a great number of grooms and other servants making enquiries in all directions.

Somebody was bound to come up with the story of a man and a woman travelling North from Meadowley.

The moon was beginning to lose its brilliance, and the stars were no longer so bright when the Duke turned in at the gates of Eagle Hall.

He reckoned that the household would not yet be awake.

This was what he wanted.

He drew up his horses outside the front-door.

A minute later the Night-footman, who must have heard them arriving, peeped out.

Then he came running down the steps.

The Duke got out of the carriage.

He drew the footman aside so that Alysia would not hear what he was saying.

"You are Henry, are you not?" he asked.

"Aye, Yer Grace. We wasn't expectin' Your Grace to be back t'night."

"I am aware of that," the Duke replied. "Now, what I want you to do, Henry, is to take the horses round to the Stables, then come back into the house and do nothing—do you understand? Do nothing until the Senior staff come on duty."

"Ye means Mr. Bates, Yer Grace?"

Bates was the Butler, and the Duke nodded.

"Yes. When Bates appears, tell him I have arrived and have a visitor with me, but on no account are we to be disturbed. Do you understand? No one is to disturb me until I ring for Danvers."

"Very good, Yer Grace. Oi'll do as ye say," Henry replied.

He was quite a bright boy.

The Duke thought it was unlikely that he would make a mistake.

He went round to the other side of the carriage. He picked Alysia up in his arms and carried her up the steps into the Hall.

He went straight on up the stairs, aware that she

was looking round her wide-eyed.

She did not speak in case he did not wish her to do so.

The Duke walked along the wide corridors with their priceless pictures and exquisite pieces of furniture.

Finally he reached the room that was next to his.

It had been his Mother's room.

When he opened the door he fancied he could still smell the fragrance of violets which was his Mother's favourite scent.

"Wait one second while I light the candelabra," he said to Alysia.

He was speaking for the first time, as he set her down on the bed.

He went back into the corridor and, taking one of the candles from a silver sconce, brought it into the room.

He lit a candelabrum which was a Cupid holding three candles.

It stood on a table by the bed.

As their light illuminated the room, Alysia asked in a nervous little voice:

"Wh-where are ... we?"

"I will tell you about it later," the Duke said. "I will go and find you something to wear. Wash away the dust, then you must get into bed."

As he spoke he walked across the room and through the communicating door at the far end which led into his own bed-room.

He thought she would very likely want to wash, and he therefore did not go back immediately, but pulled off his own coat that was covered with dust.

Then he removed the tie from around his neck.

While he was about it, he thought he would take off his other clothes which he had worn for so long.

He washed in cold water before he put on his nightshirt and a long robe.

He looked in a drawer and found a nightshirt made of the purest and finest silk, which he wore in the Summer.

He put it over his arm, then, going to the communicating door, he knocked gently.

"May I come in?" he asked.

"Y-yes . . . come in," Alysia said.

He entered the room and saw that as he had told her, she had washed the dust from her face.

She had also used his Mother's brushes and combs.

They were gold-backed and had her initials in diamonds on them. They were on the dressing-table.

Alysia had combed her hair, and it fell over her shoulders in a golden cloud.

She was in bed and had pulled the lace-edged sheet up to her neck and was holding on to it with both hands.

The Duke walked to the bed and put the white silk nightshirt in front of her.

"Put this on and go to sleep," he said. "In the morning I have a great deal to tell you, but I know now you are tired, and so am I."

"Where are we . . . staying?" Alysia asked. "It does not look like . . . an Inn!"

"Somewhere where you will be safe and where your Stepfather will not find you," the Duke replied. "The door through which I have just entered leads into my room, so if you are frightened, or if you want me, call and I will come to you."

She drew in her breath.

"You . . . you will . . . leave the door . . . open?"

"I will leave it open!" he answered. "And I shall be listening, just in case you want me."

"And . . . I really am . . . safe?" Alysia asked.

"I think you know that not only am I looking after you," the Duke said as he smiled, "but so is your Guardian Angel, who told me how to find you."

He saw Alysia's eyes light up.

"I knew you would say . . . something like . . . that," she said.

"It is something I think you have taught me to say," the Duke replied, "because I love you."

He bent down as he spoke and very gently kissed her.

It was not a kiss of passion, but of dedication.

He knew that he had brought her to his Mother's room because that was where she belonged.

"I love you, my Darling!" he said quietly.

"And . . . I love you . . . with all my . . . heart!" Alysia answered.

"Then nothing else is of any importance," the Duke said, "and we will solve all the problems to-morrow morning."

He went towards the door.

"Good-night, my Precious."

He wanted to stay, he wanted to go on kissing her, but he knew that she was exhausted.

He took one last look at her hair shining in the candlelight, and her eyes filled with love.

Then he went into his own room, leaving the communicating door open.

chapter seven

THE Duke awoke, knowing he had slept for four hours.

It had left him as fresh and alert as if he had had more rest.

He rose from his bed and walked very quietly towards the communicating door which he had left open.

He looked inside and realised that Alysia was fast asleep, so he shut the door.

He rang the bell and in a very short time Danvers, his Valet, appeared.

"Good-mornin', Y'Grace," he said cheerfully. "It's certainly a surprise to find you here. We 'ad no idea Your Grace was comin'."

"I know that, Danvers," the Duke said. "Now I have a great many things to do and I want you to listen attentively."

Danvers looked at him expectantly.

He had been with the Duke for many years.

He thought he had never seen His Grace look so young and active, as if he were enjoying life.

"First of all," the Duke began, "is Mr. Hampton here?"

"He is, Y'Grace. He arrived before dinner yesterday evenin' and brings his horse with him, that black stallion Your Grace had your eye on."

The Duke smiled.

"Then I would like to see Mr. Hampton in a few minutes," he said, "but first I wish to see Mrs. Hill."

She was the Housekeeper and Danvers, without saying any more, left the room to fetch her.

The Duke washed and had partially dressed when Danvers returned.

"Mrs. Hill's here, Y'Grace."

The Duke put on his long robe before he said:

"Show her in, Danvers, and wait outside."

Mrs. Hill was an elderly woman with greying hair. She looked very impressive, and ran the household with an iron fist.

However, everybody was fond of her, and she had been with the family for over forty years.

She was wearing the rustling black silk that was correct for her position as Housekeeper, with the silver chatelaine at her waist.

As she entered the room she dropped the Duke a curtsy.

"Good-morning, Mrs. Hill."

"Good-morning, Your Grace. It's nice to see Your Grace again. We've been looking forward to it."

"Thank you," the Duke replied, "and now I want

your help. I brought a guest home with me last night."

"As I've been told, Your Grace, and Your Grace put her in Her late Grace's bed-room!"

There was no doubt of the astonishment in the Housekeeper's voice.

"Yes, that is where I put her, and that is where she will stay," the Duke said slowly. "She has been in some trouble, Mrs. Hill, and that is why I need your help."

"You know I'm willing to do anything Your Grace wishes," Mrs. Hill replied.

"Unfortunately, the young lady was robbed by thieves of everything she possessed—her clothes, jewellery—everything—and I rescued her with some difficulty."

"I've never heard such a thing!" Mrs. Hill gasped in horror. "What a blessing Your Grace could save her."

"What I am asking is that you should provide her with clothes until we can contact Dressmakers in London and purchase some new gowns for her. I know you have a great many things hidden away in the attics."

Mrs. Hill smiled.

"I was just saying the other day, Your Grace, I've enough of your Mother's and Grandmother's belongings to fill a Museum!"

"That is what I was hoping you would say," the Duke answered. "I think Miss Alysia is about the same size as my Mother was when she was younger."

"Then it shouldn't prove too difficult, Your Grace," Mrs. Hill replied. "I'll attend to the young lady as soon as she wakes."

The Duke looked at the clock.

"There is a lot to be done," he said, "so I suggest you take her some breakfast in about two hours' time. By then you will have sorted out the clothes you consider suitable. Among other things, I wish her to have a white evening-gown which must be the most glamorous you can provide."

"I'm sure there's several to choose from," the Housekeeper answered. "Her Grace your Grandmother gave me her wedding-gown and several Court gowns to put away for her, having no further use for them."

"I am sure those will do for Miss Alysia," the Duke said, "but remember, Mrs. Hill, she has nothing—nothing at all!"

Mrs. Hill gave a little laugh.

"Isn't it just like you, Master Theo . . . I means Your Grace—to surprise us all. You always was one for the unexpected."

"You used to spoil me when I was young," the Duke said, "and I want you to spoil me now by looking after Miss Alysia. It is very important to me."

He realised the Housekeeper gave him a quick glance, but she was too well-trained to say anything.

She merely curtsied again and went from the room.

The Duke called in Danvers and sent for Harry Hampton.

He was dressed by the time Harry, in a long robe, came into his room.

"Good Heavens, Theo! I had no idea you had returned last night. Surely it is impossible—unless you ran all the way?"

"I did better than that," the Duke replied. "I drove at what I considered to be a record speed and arrived when it was still dark."

Harry looked at him. Then he said:

"You may have lost your bet, but you have a story to tell. I know by the expression on your face."

"Sit down, Harry," the Duke said, "while I tell you all that has happened."

He told Harry exactly what he had done from the moment he had left him at the Sail and Anchor.

Harry did not interrupt.

He merely sat on the edge of the bed, staring at his friend as if he could not believe what he was hearing.

The Duke finished by relating how he had stolen Alysia from her Stepfather and that she was to have been married to-day.

"If I did not know you to be completely truthful," Harry exclaimed, "I would accuse you of lying. This is a story straight out of the Book of Heroes and I can only congratulate you, Old Man, for being exceptionally clever."

He paused before he added:

"I am, however, quite sure that Maulcroft chap will try to bring a Court Action against you."

"That is what I think too," the Duke answered, "but I have the solution to that problem."

"What is that?" Harry enquired.

"I intend to marry Alysia immediately," the Duke replied, "and as it will be best to keep the wedding quiet until it has actually taken place, I want you to inform my Chaplain that I wish to be married in my Private Chapel here at midday."

Harry stared at him.

"Do you really mean that?"

"I have never been more serious in my life," the Duke replied.

"Are you really in love with this girl?"

"I doubt if you will believe me," the Duke said quietly, "but I have never been in love before."

Harry gave a whoop of joy.

"This is the best thing I have ever heard!" he exclaimed. "It is what I have always wanted for you. You were growing more cynical and more bored with every minute that passed."

"Now, we have to work quickly," the Duke said. "Maulcroft may take some time in finding me. He was quick enough the first time when he found Alysia, and I will not have her upset again."

"No, of course not," Harry said. "I will get dressed and hurry over to the Vicarage as soon as I have had my breakfast."

"If you are coming to the Breakfast-Room, I will go first and order a carriage to take you to the Vicarage," the Duke said.

"I would rather ride, and it will cause no comment. I brought *Saracen* with me, and I am delighted to be able to keep him," Harry replied.

"I suppose you are going to claim my chestnuts," the Duke remarked a little wryly.

"On the contrary," Harry answered, "I will give them to you as a wedding-present. It is cheap at the price!"

The Duke laughed as Harry went from the room and he heard him running down the corridor.

He picked up his gold watch, put it in his pocket, then walked down to the Breakfast-Room.

He knew Danvers would have already alerted the

staff that he was coming downstairs.

It was still early, and the housemaids were busy cleaning the corridors and the Hall.

The maids bobbed the Duke a curtsy as he passed and looked at him admiringly.

Because he had had so little to eat yesterday, the Duke felt hungry.

There were a dozen *entrée* dishes to choose from.

He did full justice to the hot dishes, then had some slices of ham.

It made him think of how he had enjoyed the meals he had eaten at the Inns with Alysia.

He remembered that before Mrs. Hill went to wake her, he should tell her what he had planned.

He waited until Harry had ridden off on *Saracen*.

Then he went to his bed-room and entered Alysia's through the communicating door.

The curtains were drawn and he pulled them back to let in the sunshine.

As he did so, he could hear the bees humming over the flowers and the birds singing in the bushes that were brilliant with blossom.

He had always thought that nothing was more beautiful than Eagle Hall.

He had wondered if he would ever find a woman worthy of being its Chatelaine.

The Estate had been handed down from generation to generation.

His Mother had made the garden the most spectacular in the whole county.

As he walked towards the bed, he thought he had undoubtedly found the answer.

It was impossible for anyone to look more exquisite than Alysia.

The long, slender fingers of one hand were lying on the lace-edged sheet.

Her fair hair was spread over the pillow to fall over her shoulders.

He stood looking at her eye-lashes, dark against the translucent whiteness of her skin.

He thought her little straight nose was almost Grecian and very aristocratic.

It was then the question that had been at the back of his mind began ringing in his ears.

What would his family think of his marriage?

It had been ingrained in the Duke ever since he was a small boy that his position was a very important one.

In the Social Register he ranked next to Royalty.

It was also a position of tremendous responsibility.

His Father had said to him over and over again:

"Remember, when you take my place as head of the family, that they will all look up to you and they must always respect you!"

He had put his hand on his son's shoulder before he went on:

"Promise me that you will never fail them."

The Duke could remember, and he had been only six or seven at the time, saying:

"I would never do that, Papa, and I will help, as you do, every one of our relatives who are in need."

His Father had been pleased.

The Duke thought now it was his relatives who, as soon as they learned of his marriage, would immediately ask for details of the woman he had married.

It mattered to them, and it should to him, that her blood should be the equal of his.

The Eaglefields went back to the 13th Century, and had played their part in positions of importance to every Sovereign who had reigned over England.

They had been awarded medals for Gallantry and titles that had been handed down through the family.

He was the 3rd Duke, but there had been fourteen Earls of Eagle before they had been awarded the Dukedom by King George II.

Looking down at Alysia, the Duke knew that he loved her.

He would marry her even if she had been a love-child without name.

But her Father had been a Don at Cambridge and a Professor of Languages.

He had been responsible for providing her with her very intelligent brain.

Yet the Duke was well aware that although she had money, it was no compensation for what his family would think of as a "commoner" aspiring to be his wife.

He had not missed the flicker of curiosity in Harry's eyes when he had told him who Alysia's Father was.

He had made no comment, but the Duke knew exactly what he was thinking.

'I do not care,' he thought, 'I love her and I cannot lose her. The only way I can make her safe is for her to be mine.'

They were brave words, but he was not thinking only of himself.

He knew how difficult the family could be if they thought his wife was not good enough for him.

He would protect Alysia in every way he could.

At the same time, he could not prevent the little armed barbs she would have to endure.

The comments of his women relatives would be very much the same as the Society Beauties, especially those with whom in the past he had indulged in *affairs de coeur*.

The Duchess of Eagle, if there was one, was a hereditary Lady of the Bedchamber to the Queen.

George IV was getting old.

There could be the uncomfortable suggestion that the Duchess might tactfully be asked to refuse the position when a new Queen came to the throne.

It all passed through the Duke's mind like the darkness of a nightmare.

Then the sunshine filled the room with a golden haze.

He knew then that if every King and Queen in the world tried to prevent him from marrying Alysia, he would defy them and make her his wife.

He bent and kissed her lips.

As he did so, he felt again the thrill that ran through him.

Alysia opened her eyes and he kissed her lips again.

Then he kissed her neck, and felt her quiver.

"I love you!" he said. "God, how I love you, and, my Darling, you must wake up because I have something important to tell you."

"I . . . I was . . . dreaming about you," Alysia murmured, "and I thought it could . . . only be a . . . dream . . . until you . . . kissed me."

The Duke kissed her again.

Then, as his lips became more demanding, more passionate, he deliberately controlled himself.

He sat on the bed facing her and, taking her hands in his, he kissed first one, then the other.

"You know, my Sweet," he said gently, "that I have to make certain that your wicked Stepfather can never take you from me, and there is only one way by which I can do that."

She looked at him enquiringly, her eyes seeming to fill her whole pointed face.

At the same time, he knew she was afraid because her fingers tightened on his.

"H-he is not . . . here?" she asked.

"No, of course not," the Duke said reassuringly, "but in case he should try to come here or attempt to bring any legal action against me, we are going to be married at noon."

For a moment Alysia was completely still.

Then she asked:

"Do you . . . really . . . want me?"

"I want you more than I have ever wanted anything in my whole life," the Duke said in a deep voice, "and, my Precious, I think we will be very happy."

"I shall be blissfully happy," Alysia replied. "Ever since you saved me from . . . drowning myself it has been . . . like living in . . . Wonderland."

"That is what it is going to be for the rest of our lives," the Duke said.

He thought he had never seen a woman look so radiant or so happy.

"I love you! I love you!" he said as if he could not say it too often.

He kissed her until she was breathless.

Then he said:

"Now we have to be sensible for a moment. I have

sent for my Chaplain and we will be married in the
Private Chapel. As the Duchess of Eaglefield, no one
can frighten or upset you ever again."

Alysia started at him.

"W-what . . . did you say?" she asked.

"I have not told you before," the Duke said, "but
I am in fact the Duke of Eaglefield, and this is my
home."

Alysia held on to his hand as if she were afraid of
drowning.

"H-how . . . can you be . . . so important . . . so
grand," she asked in a trembling little voice,
"and . . . still want . . . me?"

"I have already told you how much I want you,"
the Duke answered, "and I will tell you even more
convincingly once we are married."

"B-but . . ."

Alysia looked at him as if she still could not believe
what she had heard.

Then she said unexpectedly:

"Mama would be so . . . pleased. I do hope . . . she
knows I am to be . . . your wife."

"You have not mentioned your Mother's name to
me before," the Duke said, "but I shall need to know
it because, like yours, it will have to be added to my
Family Tree."

To his surprise, Alysia looked away from him.

"What is it?" he asked quickly. "What is troubling
you?"

"I am . . . just afraid that you might be . . .
as shocked at Mama for running . . . away with
Papa . . . as her parents were."

As he kissed Alysia's hand, the Duke said:

"There must be no secrets between us, my Darling. If anything is wrong, you know I would stand by you, protect you, and annihilate anybody who dares to be your enemy."

Alysia gave a little choked laugh.

"It is not as . . . bad as that . . . but Mama . . . ran away with Papa because she fell . . . in love with him when he . . . came to teach her brother . . . languages before he went to Oxford. And Papa fell in love with . . . her the . . . minute he saw . . . her."

"If she was as beautiful as you, I can understand how he felt," the Duke remarked.

"Mama was far more beautiful than I am!" Alysia replied. "In fact, she was a famous Beauty when she was a *débutante!*"

She paused before she went on nervously:

"Her Father and Mother were very . . . angry with her when she ran off with Papa because they expected her to marry . . . somebody very . . . important . . . like you."

The Duke kissed Alysia's hand again before he said:

"Tell me your Mother's name."

"She was christened Charlotte, after her Mother, who was the wife of the thirteenth Earl of Derby."

The Duke was astonished into speechlessness.

Despite her Mother's wealth, he had not imagined her to be of any social importance, considering how quietly they had lived in Meadowley.

Now he understood.

It would have been outrageous for Lady Charlotte Stanley to run away with her brother's Tutor.

But it had all happened a long time ago.

The fact that Alysia was related to one of the most

ancient and respected families in the Country was what really mattered.

The Duke's Father had always been a little jealous that the Stanley family went back to the 12th Century and was older than his own.

It all flashed through his mind.

Then he heard Alysia say in a small and frightened voice:

"You are . . . not shocked? You are . . . not going to . . . refuse to . . . marry me because . . . Mama ran away . . . like that?"

"I think it was very brave of her," the Duke replied. "You are running away, my Darling, from your evil Stepfather. But we will be as happy together as your Father and Mother were, and nothing else is of any significance."

There were tears in Alysia's eyes as she said:

"How can you . . . say anything so . . . wonderful? It is what I have always . . . prayed my husband would think . . . if I had one."

"It *is* what I think," the Duke said, "and I am quite certain, once we are married, that the present Earl of Derby, whom I have met very often on the Race Course, will welcome you to Knowlsley Park even if the last Earl refused to have your Mother there."

"My Mother used to tell me about her brothers and sisters," Alysia said. "There were quite a number of them."

She looked at the Duke, and she went on:

"She was the youngest, and because she was so beautiful, and very rich, as her Godfather had left her all his money, they expected her to marry almost as soon as she had made her curtsy to the Queen at Buckingham Palace."

"But instead she ran away with your Father," the Duke said.

"He was so handsome and so clever that I can understand how Mama must have felt, especially now that I have . . . met you!"

The Duke kissed her.

Then he said:

"Now I am going to leave you. My Housekeeper is bringing a whole wardrobe of gowns for you to choose from, and you can tell her, in secret, that you require a wedding-gown, which she has already told me she has."

He saw the excitement in Alysia's eyes as he went on:

"She will know we are going to be married today. But she is not to tell the rest of the servants."

He saw Alysia look puzzled, and he explained:

"I am taking every possible precaution against your Stepfather learning where you are until you actually belong to me and have my ring on your finger."

"You are . . . so wise . . . so clever!" Alysia said. "And please . . . Darling . . . nothing must . . . stop us from . . . being married."

She looked across the room at the open window and murmured:

"There is no balcony . . . so he cannot climb into my . . . room."

"Only I can do that," the Duke said. "Your Stepfather is too old to climb anything except a staircase, and that, I promise you, is well guarded!"

Alysia laughed.

"Let me . . . get up," she said, "and I will . . . try to look . . . beautiful for . . . you at our . . . wedding."

"You look beautiful whatever you do and whatever you wear," the Duke answered, "or whatever you do not wear!"

He was thinking of how he had seen her naked in the moonlight.

As if she followed his thoughts, she blushed, and he thought nothing could be more lovely.

With an effort he walked to the communicating door.

Even as he closed it behind him he heard a knock on the other door.

This meant, he knew, that Mrs. Hill was obeying his instructions.

He went downstairs and, a short time later, Harry came back to say that the Chaplain was on his way.

"I swore him to secrecy," Harry said. "However, I think you should have flowers in the Chapel. After all, this is the first time you have been married!"

"And the last!" the Duke said. "Very well, ask the gardeners to bring in every flower they have, but they will have to hurry. There is no need to tell them why."

"I imagine they will guess," Harry said, "but they will not have time to gossip in the village, and that, I know, is what you are afraid will happen."

"Of course it is," the Duke agreed, "because it is the law that a minor cannot marry without her Guardian's consent! But we both know that once the marriage has taken place, there will be nothing Maulcroft can do about it."

"He would be very foolish to try," Harry said. "At the same time, if you do not want your future wife to be upset, I suggest you send a message to your Gate-Keeper that he is to shut the gates and allow no one except the Chaplain to pass through them."

The Duke nodded.

"We must also tell the grooms to patrol the Park and grounds," Harry continued, "in case Maulcroft tries some other means of gaining admittance."

"He will be armed," the Duke said.

He was remembering the pistol with which Maulcroft had told Alysia he would kill him.

"Then give those you can trust a fire-arm," Harry said.

"I will leave that to you," the Duke replied.

Harry had finished his breakfast and now he got up from the table.

"I will go and see to it," he said.

The Duke, as he finished his coffee, was thinking he was glad that Harry was there.

It might be foolish, but he could not help thinking that Maulcroft would not give up so easily.

What was more, the Posting-Inns could give a description of him and say he was going to Eagle Hall.

* * *

The Duke was waiting in the Hall when, at exactly three minutes to twelve o'clock, Alysia came from her bed-room.

She was looking exquisite in a gown which had belonged to his Mother.

She had worn it at a large Reception given at Buckingham Palace, twenty years ago.

Falling on each side of her face was the delicate family veil.

It had been handed down through five generations of Eaglefield brides.

On her head was a diamond tiara.

As she came slowly down the stairs the Duke thought that no Duchess of Eaglefield had ever been more lovely.

His first thought was that he must have her portrait painted by one of the great artists.

She had reached him, and now they stood looking into each other's eyes.

The love she felt passed from Alysia's heart to the Duke's, and there was no need for words.

He offered her his arm, and she put her hand on it.

With the other hand she accepted the bouquet he handed her.

It was of small white lilies.

He thought that nothing could be more appropriate for her youth, her beauty, and her innocence.

They then made their way together along the corridors to the Chapel.

It had been part of the house ever since the reign of King Charles I.

Harry, the Duke thought, had certainly galvanised the gardeners into action.

The Chapel was massed with white flowers.

The sunshine pouring in through the stained glass windows made it all seem somehow unreal.

The Chaplain was already there, waiting in front of the altar and Harry was ready to be Best Man.

There was nobody else present.

The Chaplain, who was an elderly man, read the Marriage Service slowly and with great sincerity.

As they knelt for the blessing, Alysia felt as if the Angels were singing above them.

She was sure her Mother and Father were smiling at her happiness.

They rose to their feet and the Duke very gently kissed Alysia.

They then signed the Marriage Register which was waiting on a table near the altar.

Harry signed it as a witness, and the Chaplain said:

"May I congratulate Your Grace and may you share a happy and joyful life together which, with the Blessing of God, I am sure you will have."

"We will be very happy!" the Duke said positively.

They returned from the Chapel to one of the exquisitely furnished Sitting-Rooms.

Bates, who by this time knew what was happening, had champagne waiting for them.

Harry kissed Alysia's cheek and wished her every happiness before he said to the Duke:

"I am going to leave you now, Theo. You are on your honeymoon and I have already asked your Grandmother if I might stay with her to-night. She was curious as to why I should want to do so."

He paused to say a little apologetically:

"When I told her you were being married she was absolutely delighted and is hoping that you will find the time to take Alysia to see her either to-day or to-morrow."

"We will go after luncheon," the Duke said, "so you must stay and share it with us. I am glad, however, that for to-night, at any rate, you will be somewhere on the Estate."

The two men gave each other a meaningful glance, but they did not say anything for fear of frightening Alysia.

She was so happy that she seemed to make the whole room sparkle.

When Harry could speak to the Duke for a moment without her hearing, he said:

"Only you, Theo, could have found anything so exquisite, so absolutely, devastatingly beautiful!"

He smiled before he added:

"I still cannot believe all this has happened to you because I challenged you to walk fifty miles and find out how the ordinary man lives!"

"It is entirely due to you that I found myself 'Walking to Wonderland,'" the Duke answered. "I too can hardly believe it is true. But it has made me a different man, Harry, and the happiest you are ever likely to meet!"

"I hope to hear you saying that for the rest of your life," Harry replied.

* * *

The Duke took Alysia to meet his Grandmother in the afternoon.

She cried with joy because her beloved grandson was married at last.

"I was great friends with your Grandmother," she told Alysia, "and I remember how upset she was when her youngest daughter, who was so beautiful, ran away."

"It saddened Mama to have upset her family," Alysia said, "but she loved Papa overwhelmingly."

"And that is how you love my grandson?" the Dowager Duchess asked.

"With all my heart!" Alysia answered softly.

"That is all I want to hear," the Dowager Duchess said, "and I intend to write to your uncle, who is now the Earl of Derby. I know when I tell him how sweet and lovely you are, he will want to meet you."

Alysia kissed the Dowager Duchess.

"Thank you!" she said. "I know that would please Mama. She always regretted that I could not attend Balls and be as grand as she was when she was a girl."

"You will be very grand from now on," the Dowager Duchess smiled.

"Please, will you help me?" Alysia begged. "I shall need your help because I am so frightened I might do something which will make Theo ashamed of me in some way."

The Duke knew how touched his Grandmother was at Alysia's request.

He thought no-one could be so hard-hearted as to refuse to help her.

"I am lucky, so very lucky!" he told himself.

The Duke thought the same thing later.

After a candlelit dinner in the *Boudoir* which opened out of his mother's bed-room he picked Alysia up and carried her into his.

There was no maid in attendance.

He kissed her all the time he was undressing her, until finally she slipped into the great four-poster bed.

He joined her and felt her soft body quivering against him.

He knew then he had almost reached the point of ecstasy.

It was not only physical, but very spiritual.

He knew he had to be very gentle with Alysia because she was so young and innocent.

But he also knew that, to her, he was not just a man but someone sent to her by God.

Love was Divine and so was he.

"I love you . . . I . . . love you!" Alysia was whispering.

Then he was kissing her until they seemed to travel up to the stars that had shone over them last night.

They became one with the moon which had guided them to safety.

It was perfect.

They felt it not only with their hearts, but also with their souls.

The Duke knew it was something he could never express in words.

He could only feel as if Alysia had opened the Gates of Heaven for him.

* * *

It was very much later that night when Alysia moved against his shoulder that he asked:

"I have made you happy, my precious love?"

"So happy . . . that I am sure . . . I will . . . wake up to find it is all a dream . . . and you are not really there."

"I shall always be here," the Duke vowed, "always, always!"

Even as he spoke he heard a shot ring out, followed by another.

Both he and Alysia were suddenly motionless.

"D-did you . . . hear that?" she asked nervously.

"I did," the Duke answered.

He got out of bed, put on his robe, and went to the window.

He could see nothing.

But the window looked out onto the back of the Hall, and he knew he must go to the front.

"I must go and see what is happening," he said.

Alysia gave a little cry as he opened the door and ran down the stairs.

The front-door was already open and the two Night-footmen were on the steps outside.

The Duke joined them.

"What has happpened?" he asked.

"Two shots, Y'Grace," one of the footmen answered, "an' Oi sees a man fall orf 'is 'orse."

The Duke was looking towards the great oak trees in the Park.

Then he saw somebody come riding along from under the trees and across the bridge that spanned the lake.

He stood very still, then he gave an exclamation of relief.

As the horse and rider came nearer, he realised he was right in thinking it was Harry.

Harry rode up to the steps and, without dismounting, said:

"I expected that swine would turn up to-night, so I joined the grooms who were looking out for him. He shot at me, obviously thinking I was you, and I returned his fire."

The Duke thought it was very likely that Maulcroft had mistaken Harry for himself.

It was something that had happened in the past.

Maulcroft, who had never seen him, had doubtless had a description.

"He is dead?" the Duke asked.

"He is still breathing, but I shot him close to the heart and it is only a question of hours," Harry replied. "The grooms are taking him to the Doctor in the village. I think he will be dead before morning."

"I am very grateful to you," the Duke said seriously. "This is another debt I owe you."

"It is going to prove an expensive wedding-present!" Harry joked. "I think now, Theo, I should go and tell the Chief Constable what has happened. I know he lives about two miles away, and the sooner that damned man is dead and buried, the better!"

"I agree with you," the Duke answered. "Thank you again. Come and see me after you have had some sleep."

"I will do that," Harry said.

He rode off and the Duke went back upstairs.

Alysia was sitting up in bed, waiting for him, and she was obviously very agitated.

"It is all right, my precious," the Duke said reassuringly. "Your Stepfather will never worry you again."

"He is . . . dead? Can it really be . . . true?"

"He fired at Harry, who fired back in self-defence."

"Then there can be no scandal about it . . . can there?" Alysia asked.

"None at all," the Duke answered. "He was intruding on private property and it will be thought he deserved what happened to him."

To his consternation, Alysia burst into tears.

The Duke held her close.

"Do not cry, my lovely one," he pleaded.

"I . . . I thought he might . . . hurt . . . you. I was so afraid that . . . because I had . . . married you my Stepfather . . . would kill you . . . and it would be . . . my fault."

"There is nothing he can do in the future," the Duke said quietly, "but thank you, my Darling, for worrying about me and wanting to protect me."

"Of course . . . I want to . . . protect you," Alysia said. "I want to look . . . after you and . . . love you for . . . ever and ever. But I might have . . . brought you . . . bad luck."

"Instead of which I am the luckiest man in the world, as I told Harry earlier," the Duke said. "I have found somebody I love and whom I shall love more and more every day of my life."

Alysia looked up at him, tears on her cheeks.

"I love you with all my heart and with all . . . my soul . . . and of course . . . my brain!"

The Duke chuckled.

"I adore all three of them," he said, "and also something else."

"What . . . is that?" Alysia asked.

"Your beautiful, exquisite body, and that is mine too."

"Everything of . . . mine is . . . yours," Alysia whispered passionately.

Then the Duke's lips were on hers and he was holding her closer and closer still.

There were no tears, no more fears as they flew away into the Wonderland that was all their own.

ABOUT THE AUTHOR

Barbara Cartland, the world's most famous romantic novelist, who is an historian, playwright, lecturer, political speaker and television personality, has now written over 570 books and sold over 650 million copies all over the world.

She has also had many historical works published and has written four autobiographies as well as the biographies of her mother and that of her brother, Ronald Cartland, who was the first Member of Parliament to be killed in the last war. This book has a preface by Sir Winston Churchill and has just been republished with an introduction by Sir Arthur Bryant.

Love at the Helm, a novel written with the help and inspiration of the late Earl Mountatten of Burma, Great Uncle of His Royal Highness The Prince of Wales, is being sold for the Mountbatten Memorial Trust.

She has broken the world record for the last seventeen years by writing an average of twenty-three books a year. In the *Guiness Book of World Records* she is listed as the world's top-selling author.

Miss Cartland in 1978 sang an Album of Love Songs with the Royal Philharmonic Orchestra.

In private life Barbara Cartland, who is a Dame of the Order of St. John of Jerusalem, President of the St. John Council in Hertfordshire and Deputy President of the St. John Ambulance Brigade, has fought for better conditions and salaries for Midwives and Nurses.

She championed the cause for the Elderly in 1956, invoking a Government Enquiry into the "Housing Conditions of Old People."

In 1962 she had the Law of England changed so that Local Authorities had to provide camps for their own Gypsies. This has meant that since then thousands and thousands of Gypsy children have been able to go to school, which they had never been able to do in the past, as their caravans were moved every twenty-four hours by the Police.

There are now fourteen camps in Hertfordshire and Barbara Cartland has her own Romany Gypsy Camp called Barbaraville by the Gypsies.

Her designs "Decorating with Love" are being sold all over the U.S.A. and the National Home Fashions League made her, in 1981, "Woman of Achievement."

She is unique in that she was one and two in the Dalton list of Best Sellers, and one week had four books in the top twenty.

Barbara Cartland's book *Getting Older, Growing Younger* has been published in Great Britain and the U.S.A. and her fifth cookery book, *The Romance of Food*, is now being used by the House of Commons.

In 1984 she received at Kennedy Airport America's Bishop Wright Air Industry Award for her contribution to the development of aviation. In 1931 she and two R.A.F. Officers thought of, and carried, the first aeroplane-towed glider airmail.

During the war she was Chief Lady Welfare Officer in Bedfordshire looking after 20,000 Service men and women. She thought of having a pool of Wedding Dresses at the War Office so a Service Bride could hire a gown for the day.

She bought 1,000 gowns without coupons for the A.T.S., the W.A.A.F's and the W.R.E.N.S. In 1945 Barbara Cartland received the Certificate of Merit from Eastern Command.

In 1964 Barbara Cartland founded the National Association for Health of which she is the President, as a front for all the Health Stores and for any product made as alternative medicine.

This is now a £65 million turnover a year, with one-third going in export.

In January 1988 she received a *La Médaille de Vermeil de la Ville de Paris*. This is the highest award to be given in France by the City of Paris. She has sold 25 million books in France.

Barbara Cartland was received with great enthusiasm by her fans, who fêted her at a reception in the City, and she received the gift of an embossed plate from the Government.

In March 1988 Barbara Cartland was asked by the Indian Government to open their Health Resort outside Delhi. This is almost the largest Health Resort in the world.

Barbara Cartland was made a Dame of the Order of the British Empire in the 1991 New Year's Honours List by Her Majesty, The Queen, for her contribution to Literature and also for her years of work for the community.

AWARDS

1945   Received Certificate of Merit, Eastern Command.

1953   Made a Commander of the Order of St. John of Jerusalem. Invested by H.R.H. The Duke of Gloucester at Buckingham Palace.

1972   Invested as Dame of Grace of the Order of St. John in London by the Lord Prior, Lord Cacia.

1981   Received "Achiever of the Year" from the National Home Furnishing Association in Colorado Springs, U.S.A.

1984   Received Bishop Wright Air Industry Award at Kennedy Airport, for inventing the aeroplane-towed glider.

1988   Received from Monsieur Chirac, The Prime Minister, the Gold Medal of the City of Paris, at the Hotel de la Ville, Paris.

1991   Invested as Dame of the Order of The British Empire, by H.M. The Queen at Buckingham Palace.